KILLING BARDOE

Also by Keith Remer

The Hiding Place of Thunder

KILLING BARDOE

BOOK ONE OF
THE CALAMITOUS BREED
TRILOGY

by

KEITH REMER

Honey Lee Press
Oklahoma City, Oklahoma

The Calamitous Breed

First Honey Lee Press trade paperback edition March 2018
Manufactured in the United States of America
10 9 8 7 6 5 4 3 2 1

Print ISBN 978-0-9998532-0-7
EBook ISBN 978-0-9998532-1-4
Library of Congress Control Number: 2018901108

For my father,
Lester C. Remer,

who instilled in me a love

for the western genre.

Oklahoma Territory, 1893

CHAPTER ONE

A Damned Raw Deal

The two young men devoured meals from the rough-hewn table top since their toddler days. Now the two youngest Mosier brothers lay in display, side by side, on the old table. Davy endured life as the baby of the family. The .41 caliber slug, still buried deep in the back of his head, deformed a face once considered handsome. Jake lived in the world two years before Davy came out screaming. A worn but freshly cleaned cotton shirt with a banded collar concealed the grisly evidence of Davy's gaping chest wounds.

Bob Mosier stood alongside Ma and Pa Mosier and thought the neighbor women did a fair piece of work preparing his brothers for viewing. Bob didn't believe he'd ever seen the boys' hands and faces scrubbed so clean.

"I wish they'd listened to me," Bob said shaking his head. "I was only gone an hour, but I told them both to keep a close eye on that Dallas Babb."

"I wish they hadn't been outlaws," Ma Mosier responded. Few tears ever spilled from the old woman's eyes. Life in the Oklahoma Territory turned her too hard for out and out crying, but her gnarled hands gripped and wrung at the hem of a stained apron. "I didn't raise my boys to be outlaws," she added, "but that's what every one of ya'll become."

Pa Mosier didn't say a word. He seldom offered comment on any topic, but he did nod his head in agreement with his wife's words. And Bob nodded his as well.

Neither Ma nor Pa had anything to do with Bob and the two younger boys going bad. Their oldest boy, Leroy, shoved his younger brothers toward evil. Bob, Jake and young Davy just followed the lead of their big brother and all went astray as a result. Bob didn't know what made Leroy go bad. The best he could figure, Leroy came out of the womb that way. And everyone agreed Leroy Mosier far exceeded his younger brothers' talents for doing wrong.

Bob's stomach ached at the mere thought of his older brother. Leroy would be coming through the door soon, and he surely would not be pleasant. Dallas Babb not only killed his kin, but also rode away with every single cent he and the Mosier boys stole from the Farmers Citizens Bank up in Ponca City. Leroy spent the last week in Henryetta with a favorite whore, celebrating the success of his bank-robbing ways. Bob sent a telegraph to him late afternoon the day before and now Leroy Mosier rode hell bent for leather to reach the little homestead south of Stillwater in Oklahoma Territory.

It didn't take him long. Bob and his old mama and daddy still stood around the table when Leroy Mosier threw open the door to the rickety cabin and stepped inside. He nodded a greeting to his parents before stepping up close to the table holding the bodies of his youngest brothers. Leroy shook his head and emitted a grunt, but didn't bother removing his flat topped hat with the wide and drooping brim.

"I told 'em to keep a close eye on Dallas... " Bob started before Leroy cut him off sharply.

"Shut your lips, Bob."

Bob did just that, but Ma Mosier showed no appreciation for her oldest boy's temperament. "This is all your doings, Leroy Mosier," she said with her eyelids narrowed to mere slits.

Leroy stared at the aging matriarch for a hard, long second and then seemed to say something other than what he intended. "Damn… couldn't you have laid them out somewheres other than where we eat?"

"I ain't heard no one say you'd ever be eatin' at my table again anyhow," Ma said.

"Now, Old Woman, don't be puttin' out words you don't mean," Pa mumbled.

Leroy's lips snarled beneath his bushy mustache as he mocked, "Yeah…You listen to your husband, Ma."

Bob expected his mama to say more, but she didn't, and they all watched as Leroy stepped up to the feet of the once young and now dead Davy. Leroy and Davy inherited Pa's tall stature and large feet, and the boots on Davy's feet looked in much better shape than the ones Leroy wore. The oldest brother removed the boots from the youngest brother's feet.

"Ain't no sense in putting such good leather in a grave," Leroy said as a simple matter of fact.

Bob couldn't help but notice the neighbor women didn't bother with his little brother's feet. They obviously hadn't seen a washing in a month of Sundays. It kind of tugged at Bob's heart how his mama picked up her oldest son's discarded battered boots and tenderly put them on the grimy feet of her baby boy.

Leroy turned his attention to Bob. "Where are your guns?"

Leroy sported a holstered Colt Peacemaker and a hammerless Smith and Wesson tucked into the waist band of his wool trousers.

"Why, Leroy, I hadn't seen no call in wearing my guns to a funeral," Bob explained.

"You ain't going to be at no funeral," Leroy growled. "You and me got a dirty scoundrel to run down. We got to find that Dallas Babb before he spends all our hard earned money. "

Bob hurried to get his weaponry but still overheard the exchange between his daddy and only remaining brother.

"I best get a shovel and get my two youngest in the ground."

"Yeah, guess you better, Pa. These boys aren't long from starting to swell and stink."

****

Leroy and Bob Mosier's horses carried them a good ways from the little cabin before the oldest decided to speak. "Guess Babb shot them both from behind?"

"Didn't look that way to me, Leroy," Bob grimaced. "From finding them, I gathered that Babb took Jake head on and put two slugs in his chest. Looked to me as if Davy had tried to pull foot out of there and Dallas took a good bead and put a bullet in the back of his head. You know what a shootist that boy is... having been trained by one of the very best and all."

Leroy grunted his doubt before replying, "We'll find out just how good he is when we catch up with him."

Bob didn't say anything else. He knew not to talk to Leroy in times like this until Leroy showed a need for talk. Bob didn't presently know their destination. He just followed. It seemed to him as if he'd spent a lifetime just following the eldest Mosier.

The brothers were still a good piece from Stillwater when they rode upon Mack Wade and the simple-minded half-breed everyone knew only as Charlie.

Wade and Charlie approached from the opposite direction. They tugged on their reins and Wade spoke first.

"I hear Dallas Babb done killed a couple of you Mosier brothers. Wasn't sure which ones, but I guess it wasn't you two."

"You'd be guessing right," Leroy growled. "What business is it of yours?"

"Well," Wade drawled and coupled with an easy grin, "I also hear he might have some money that you'd be wanting back. Me and Charlie here wouldn't mind lending a hand for just a little bit of that money."

Bob felt some relief when Leroy didn't seem immediately opposed to taking on help. The thought of four men going up against Dallas Babb kind of soothed an ache gnawing at Bob's innards. Babb could damned sure shoot a revolver – a show off if there ever was one. On the other hand, Bob and his older brother couldn't shoot all that good. They could both hit the broad side of a barn, but they best stand darn near the barn. Leroy didn't believe it necessary to shoot well. He just strived to get up close and throw out as much lead as humanly possible in the least amount of time. That practice would not work now against Dallas Babb. He'd drop either Mosier before they got within fifty feet of him. Babb required surrounding and flushing out, and two more hands made that an easier job to get done. The two men sitting their horses across from the Mosier brothers would do well for surrounding and flushing.

Bob knew Wade's reputation as a mean son of a bitch and believed the slightly cross-eyed Charlie more than just half crazy. Some said Charlie's brains made him only as smart as a slow twelve-year-old, but the half white and half Choctaw idiot could work ugly wonders with the bowie knife sheathed in the wide belt around his waist. He also could skillfully apply the Winchester draped across his lap.

Leroy didn't get in any hurry taking Wade up on his offer. Bob started getting jittery when his brother finally said, "You say you will pitch in with us for a little bit of money. What's a little bit of money?"

"Well, now that depends," Wade nodded. "Are you just wanting your money back, or do you aim to punish Babb for his murderous ways?"

"We aim to kill the bastard," Leroy snorted.

"You'd have to give us a hundred a piece to throw in on a killin'," Wade said.

"I won't kick about that amount. You got yourself a deal."

Leroy and Mack Wade leaned out from their saddles to shake on the agreement.

****

Dallas Babb awakened from a midday's nap to find himself staring up and into the barrels of two double-barreled shotguns. An old man and a young boy aimed down at him and Babb didn't know which he felt most of... embarrassment... or anger.

Embarrassed because he was *Dallas Babb* and here he lay on the ground outgunned by a couple of hayseeds; angry at himself for letting his guard down, and angry at these two for kicking him awake in the middle of the day to shove their squirrel guns in his face.

"You are on our property," the old man barked.

"Hell, I was just napping," Dallas offered.

"We been looking at you while you was a sleeping and we reckon we know who you are," the old man said.

"Well, who do you reckon I be then?" Babb mocked.

"We saw your picture in the post office. You're that Dallas Babb."

Babb laughed a response. "Hell, my name ain't Babb. My name is Smith."

The boy then spoke in a voice betraying fear. "Gramps, I told you we should have shot him in his sleep."

Babb turned his coldest glare on the boy. "Shoot a man while he's sleeping? Why hell, boy, that's a damned raw deal."

Dallas Babb always kept both handguns concealed. A derringer hid in a hip pocket holster. He kept the much larger .41 caliber Colt closer to his heart.

The granddaddy held his shotgun steady. Both barrels of the boy's weapon swayed with every beat of his young heart.

"Mister," the old man said, "I ain't never shot a man in his sleep and I don't intend to start now. But you as much as twitch and I'll let go with both barrels of this here ten gauge."

Babb showed the palms of both hands to the grandfather. "Paps, I got papers in my breast pocket proving that my name is Smith and not Babb. Will you let me retrieve them?"

"Move easy," the old man agreed with a nod.

Dallas Babb slowly moved his right hand into the left side of his frock coat and released the Colt from his shoulder rig. He brought it out quick and put a single bullet right smack between the old man's eyes.

The boy let go of his shotgun and it hit the earth about the same time as did his grand pappy.

"You done killed my gramps," the boy exclaimed. Tears instantly welled in his eyes and a moment later a wet spot spread across the crotch of his bibbed overalls.

"How old are you, boy?" Babb asked calmly.

"I'm only fourteen," the boy sobbed.

Babb grinned and shook his head. "Hell, I was fourteen when I learned to shoot. I'm only twenty now, but just the other day I killed my first two, boy. Do you have any idea how it feels in your heart to take a man's life with your very own hands?"

"No, sir," the boy babbled.

"It don't feel all that bad," Babb chuckled. He put his next round in the boy's heart.

****

The Mosier boys and their two new pards spent the rest of the day combing the backwoods outside Stillwater. They checked most of their haunts and hiding places in that vicinity, and Bob Mosier drew damned saddle weary. He sighed and slumped in relief when Leroy stopped and said they would camp for the night.

Wade and Charlie tended their horses as Leroy pulled Bob aside.

"Bob, you noticed how that breed's been eyeing you all day?"

Bob thought his mind had been playing tricks on him. Now he realized maybe he hadn't just imagined Charlie paying him a good deal of attention.

"Yeah, I noticed."

"Word has it that he'll take his pleasure with either a man or a woman, and it don't matter which to him. You best keep an eye on him tonight."

"Leroy," Bob choked, "are you joshing me?"

"Bob, I wouldn't josh about my only remaining brother being sodomized by a crazy half-breed."

Bob Mosier didn't sleep a wink that night.

CHAPTER TWO

Mr. Store Keep

"I'm thinking you should just stay here with me on this lovely morning. Let the general store be closed, and you and I will simply frolic the day away."

Clay Bardoe stared at his beautiful bride of two years while choosing the practical words of his mind over those stirred by his heart. "We inherited that store from your daddy. You like to tell that he never missed one single day of being open for business. Millie, I have a tradition to uphold."

Millicent Bardoe feigned indignation as she pushed away from the kitchen table to clear the breakfast dishes. "So be it, Clay. You just go right on and choose your occupation over the love of your life. I will just stay here to slave away in my gardens and anxiously await your return."

"You be careful in those gardens. Both the copperheads and the rattlers seem to be especially abundant this year."

Millie turned with a handful of plates to beam a magnificent smile at her man.

"Why, Clay Bardoe, without even knowing it, you have just expressed profound love and concern for me. I would have rather heard it in straightforward English, but I will take the sentimental tidbits you offer."

"Millie," Bardoe grinned wearily, "you know I love you."

"I know you do, Clay. You just don't say it often enough with your lips, and when you do, you don't do so with the exuberance I know you feel. Alas, I am forced to look to your actions to declare that you love *me* more than you love life itself!"

"Keep an eye out for the snakes," Bardoe said dryly while wishing he could instead *exuberantly* tell this woman of the wonders he held for her in his heart. Although he had learned the occupation of the refined and gentler types, Bardoe had not learned to chatter on the contents of his soul.

"Pshaw!" Millie huffed as she abandoned the dramatic for her more natural state of feistiness. "It was I that nursed you back from the very brink of death, was it not?"

"It sure enough was," Bardoe smiled.

"Well then I'm certain I could tend to my doctoring should I get bitten by a nasty old snake."

"The problem is," Bardoe said as he took his wife in his arms for a hug and goodbye kiss, "that nasty old snakes don't tend to travel alone and they strike multiple times."

Two miles stretched between Bardoe's home and his store in Stillwater. On this lovely morning Clay Bardoe made the hike with the blue of Millie's eyes, the golden sheen of her hair, and brilliance of her smile dancing with the very beat of his heart.

****

Leroy Mosier revealed his plan to the makeshift gang while they sat around their morning campfire. Bob often did not agree with his brother, but didn't often say anything about it. This morning Bob suffered a cranky state of mind for a lack of sleep, and it put him off his mark. Charlie continued eyeballing him as well, and that too tended to push Bob uncharacteristically to challenge Leroy.

"I don't like it," Bob said with a shake of his head. "Hell, Leroy, we'd just be playing with fire and tempting it to burn us."

Leroy Mosier's mustached lip curled into a snarl. "Are you the leader of this here posse?"

"Is that what we are, Leroy? A posse?" Bob asked.

"We are going out to deliver justice to a murderer and a thief. That is exactly what we are. Now, are you the leader of this here posse?"

Bob emitted a loud sigh before admitting, "Naw... I ain't its leader."

"Then you don't have to like it. You just have to do it. And if you can't do it, then you just need to ride on out of here," Leroy said.

Bob's face glowed a deeper red than the campfire coals even before Charlie jumped in.

"I think you jest skeer'd. Ain't ya? Ain't ya jest skeer'd?"

Bob pretty much had all Charlie he wanted already. The way the loon looked at him, and the way his one eye kind of crossed all started to mount up on Bob. The thought entered his mind to just pull his gun and gut-shoot Charlie while he least expected it. But then Bob would have to quickly turn the gun on Wade and shoot or be shot. However, if Bob shot them both right here and now, it'd put a real damper on Leroy's plans, and Leroy would not respond in a favorable manner. Instead of shooting, Bob provided Charlie an answer.

"There ain't nothin' wrong with a man being afeared of some thing or someone that can do him great harm."

"Hell, I ain't skeer'd," Charlie sneered with the one crossed eye just twitching. "I ain't skeer'd of a blamed thang. If'n the devil hisself was to walk into this camp, I'd jump up..."

Which Charlie did.

"... and I'd pull this here Arkansas toothpick from my belt... "

Which Charlie did.

"... and I'd holler, 'Hey you old devil, come on over here so I can cut your balls off!'"

Leroy and Buck Wade broke out in hearty laughter. Bob, however, didn't find a damned thing funny about the half Choctaw, half white man, and whole idiot who went by only one name.

****

Clay Bardoe stocked a newly arrived shipment of medicinal items on his shelves when the little bell on the front door jingled an alert that someone likely to have spending money just stepped onto the premises. Bardoe turned from the shelves to learn that it wasn't someone normally in the disposition or position to make a purchase with cash money. It was just his older sister, Lyle Babb. Lyle moved herself and her son to Stillwater shortly after Bardoe and Millicent relocated to the town in order to take over Millie's family interests. Lyle often professed she'd only done so to be closer to a brother she'd never had the opportunity to be close to.

"Clay, I need your help and I need it badly!" Lyle said in a voice shrill from the burden of yet another catastrophe befalling her pitiful existence.

Bardoe and Lyle held little in common. She married badly at a young age, and accomplished next to nothing ever since.

"What's the problem, Lyle?" Bardoe asked while fighting off the urge to add

" ...this time." While they shared little in common, Bardoe did not wish her ill or intend to cause her additional misery.

"It's Dallas, Clay. It's my beloved only son."

Bardoe could have guessed as much.

"You know the law is after him and those worthless Mosier boys for robbing a bank in Ponca City?"

"Yeah, I know that."

"Now I hear tell Dallas shot and killed two of them brothers and the remaining two are out to kill my boy. Now,

Clay, you know if Dallas *did* shoot down those Mosiers... they must have had it coming."

Bardoe knew no such thing, but admitting as much would serve no purpose.

"Clay, now Dallas has the law, the Mosier brothers, and who knows how many bounty hunters after him. You got to go to him and help him out of this terrible predicament."

Bardoe took a deep breath and moved to a position closer to his portly sister. Her graying hair looked a mess beneath her bonnet, and her eyes revealed the tell-tale redness of tears already shed.

"Oh, Lyle, even if I knew where to find Dallas, there would be not a thing I could do to help him out of this mess. Let's say I was to find him, all I could do is suggest that he turn himself in, and you know he isn't about to do that."

"You could stand up beside him, Clay. You could help him fight his way out of this territory and make his escape."

It pained Bardoe, but here he had to lay it out straight to his sister. "You know I wouldn't do that."

"It was you that taught him to shoot, Clay Bardoe!" Lyle practically growled.

"I did teach him to shoot. I didn't teach him to kill."

"You killed men, Clay!" Lyle's eyes narrowed to hateful slits.

"There the record is wrong. I've shot men, but I never killed one. I intentionally never killed any of them."

"Glory be, Clay," Lyle hissed, "with the skills you once possessed, you are going to let them hunt down and kill your own flesh and blood?"

"Lyle, I have shelves to stock."

Bardoe felt no triumph in his sister leaving his store in an all-fired pucker. In truth, he pitied the woman for having produced such a no-account for a son.

****

Bardoe toiled at his work not near long enough when the little bell jingled again. This time the jangling of two sets of spurs accompanied the bell's jingle. Bardoe could not view the front door from his position on the ladder. He descended as a booming voice rang out at his back.

"I think I know you, store keep!"

Bardoe had not heard that voice in nearly three years, but recognized it immediately, and it brought a fond smile to his lips. He walked around the corner of a tall cabinet to find the owner of the deep baritone voice leaning against the store counter. A younger man stood at his side.

"Howdy, CB Wooly," Bardoe said with his wide smile still intact.

Wooly smiled back but seemed to ignore the greeting. Instead, he lightly elbowed the man at his side.

"Say, Walt," Wooly grinned to the man beside him, "would you believe that that man standing to our front in that awfully clean white cotton shirt and woolen trousers and brogan shoes is the famed Clay Bardoe?"

The man named Walt had clearly been schooled by Wooly. "Why no, CB, I wouldn't believe that at all. I always heard Clay Bardoe was partial to silk shirts and fine stove top boots with a coffin toe. I heard he never went anyplace without a light colored Stetson with a Montana peak and knife-blade brim."

"I do swear, Walt, that peaceful clerk of a man does look like my old partner Clay Bardoe. Of course… " CB Wooly paused to dramatically stare at Clay's waist with deeply squinted eyelids. "… I don't see those pearl handled .45's that he wore cross-draw in Slim Jim holsters."

CB Wooly straightened and walked within hand shaking distance of Bardoe. "So, tell me, Mr. Store Keep, could you possibly be the one and the only Deputy United States Marshal Clay Bardoe?"

Bardoe shook his head and chuckled. It brought comfort to know that some people never changed. He stuck out his hand and said, "It's good to see you, CB."

"It's been too long, Clay," Wooly said as he enthusiastically pumped Bardoe's hand.

Bardoe looked long and hard at the badge on Wooly's chest. It stirred something deep within him. "I heard a while back that you're now tracking outlaws for the newly appointed federal judge over in Guthrie. Hell, you've been wrangling outlaws for a good many years now, CB."

"Probably too many, Clay, but what else would I do? Heck, we can't all marry beautiful women and inherit both her daddy's house and store!"

Bardoe knew Wooly didn't mean any offense, but the truth did pack a sting. Bardoe hadn't exactly hand-picked the route leading to Millie and her father's good fortune.

CB Wooly pointed to the man still standing back by the counter. "Clay, I want you to meet my partner, Walt Tabor. Walt, meet Clay Bardoe."

The young deputy stepped up and shook Bardoe's hand, "This is a real honor for me, Mr. Bardoe. You're somewhat of a living legend among our ranks."

"Somewhat?" Wooly howled before Bardoe could offer a response.

"Hell, boy, there wasn't a deputy marshal in any territory more famous than this man... "

Wooly went on while Tabor displayed a good nature with a friendly grin. He struck Bardoe as the kind of man he would choose to ride with. As Wooly brought up memories probably best left to the past, all Bardoe could do was just roll his eyes and shake his head in embarrassment.

"... The best known fact about old Clay is he never shot to kill. Our times didn't produce another man like that. Take me for instance, Walt. Heck fire, when it comes down to having to shoot, I'll just shoot at a man's broadest body part...be that his gut or be that his ass! I don't necessarily shoot to kill; I just shoot to hit, and if'n the rascal dies in the process, well so be it," he grinned.

"Yet, Clay here," Wooly continued, "he was so good with a revolver, he could just pick a point on a man's body that he wanted to put a bullet in. It might have been a wrist, or an ankle, or elbow, or hell, Clay might just decide to shoot off some old boy's ear! I never saw him once miss anything he was shooting at."

"You must not been looking close enough then, CB," Bardoe butted in.

"Hogwash!" Wooly thundered. "You always aimed to wound, and you always hit what you aimed at. Now I will tell you, Walt, that practice did come back to bite ol' Clay in the ass! Didn't it, Clay?"

"It sure enough did, CB," Bardoe grimaced.

Bardoe did not wish to be rude, and remained cordial, but would rather have not reheard the telling of a bad day in his history. He just reminded himself that in the end, it all turned out for the best.

"Walt, several years back we'd run down a sorry son of a bitch by the name of Elvin Timms, and he just would not go peaceful like. It turned out Clay found it necessary to shoot Timms in the right shoulder. Clay just knew Timms would either hang or spend the rest of his sorry life in prison. It didn't happen that way did it, Clay?"

"Nope, it didn't happen that way, CB."

"Nope. The jury let Timms go. Three weeks later, Clay is walking down a peaceful side street in Fort Smith, when

Timms steps around a corner behind Clay and puts three slugs right in the middle of his back."

Wooly put a hand on Clay's shoulder and cocked his head at Walt Tabor. "Clay spent six months in a Fort Smith hospital. Nearly died more times than I can count. Probably would have died for sure, had there not been a pretty little nurse there named Millicent. Now, that girl's his wife, and here's old Clay Bardoe running a general store. Now tell me, Walt, don't that beat all?"

"It beats all, CB," Tabor agreed.

Bardoe nodded his own agreement. It did in fact beat all. It would make an even better story if Wooly told the portion that exemplified his very own legend.

While Bardoe lay up in that hospital, his partner ruthlessly tracked Timms night and day for nearly two weeks. Wooly caught up with the back shooting bastard near Fort Gibson in Indian Territory, and at close range emptied both barrels of a double-barreled shotgun into his face. Bardoe never doubted that Wooly done this more out of friendship than a sense of duty, and Bardoe never intended to forget the old friend's loyalty.

Both men took a few moments to chew silently on the past events living themselves out once again in their minds. Wooly broke the silence.

"Clay, I wish this was in its entirety a social calling, but it ain't."

"I figured as much, CB."

"It's your nephew, Dallas Babb. We got warrants for his arrest."

"I figured that much as well."

"Don't guess you'd know where we'd find the boy?"

"I have no idea."

They reached the point where a lawman would stare squint-eyed at any person who said they didn't know the whereabouts of kin. CB Wooly naturally spared Bardoe the insult.

"Clay, I hear tell you taught young Dallas how to shoot."

"Regrettably… that I did."

Wooly took a moment or two to consider the ramifications and then expressed his deductions by shaking his head and clucking his tongue. Then he once again offered his right hand to Bardoe.

"Ol' friend, I doubt the boy will come looking for us, so we must go looking for him. It was damned good seeing you again."

Bardoe agreed it had been pleasant, and he waved a good-bye to Walt Tabor. Before stepping out the door, Wooly turned once more toward Bardoe.

"Clay, something I've always wondered and feel a hunger to ask. When you decided never to put a badge back on your chest, was it because of your love for Millicent, or because those three bullets gave you a newfound respect for death?"

"I'm no stranger to that question, CB. I've asked the same thing of myself."

"And what was your answer, old pard?"

"Why, CB... it was for both reasons. I care too deeply for Millicent to do anything that might shorten the time we have together."

Wooly nodded his acceptance of the response, tipped the brim of his hat and started again for the door.

Bardoe spoke up this time. "CB, all this sentimental talk has suddenly made me feel obliged to warn that Dallas Babb might possibly have surpassed the skills of his teacher and, too, he's a killer."

CB Wooly walked out of the store shaking his head and clucking his tongue.

CHAPTER THREE

Large and Jagged Holes

Millicent could busy her hands, but her mind stayed on the man she loved. Clay Bardoe proved to be one of a kind and worthy of every single second she spent dwelling on him. She still considered Clay a work in progress, but he had indeed changed so much from the rough and tumble law man she first fell immediately in love with. His changes came gradually, but they did come and showed mostly in his eyes. In the Fort Smith hospital long ago, the eyes betrayed a heart bent toward a life of violence. During the couple's few precious years together his eyes softened to reflect a nature refined by affection. Millie loved Clay Bardoe intensely, and in his eyes she observed duplication or maybe even magnification of that intensity. What her Clay could not force his tongue to convey, his wonderful eyes could not conceal.

Millie initially doubted a man of adventure could find satisfaction as a husband and mere proprietor of a general store. However, that he did. The circumstances did not fool Millie into thinking it anything less than a profound love for her which turned Clay from a life of violence to a life of keeping a store and maintaining a marriage.

His previous life lay buried in a trunk up in the attic of her ancestral home – now their home. A hat, boots, Colt revolvers, and even a long coat bearing horrible scars, rested hopefully forever out of sight and out of commission. Millie hoped her man might one day climb the stairs to the attic for no other reason than to remove the trunk and surrender it to a blazing fire, signifying he would never again have need of such.

Until that day, Millie intended to do nothing more than shower Clay with unconditional devotion. After all, it came so easy and found its way back to her tenfold. Millicent Bardoe seemed guaranteed of a long and wonderful life with a man who although could not say it in words, believed her to be the very reason his heart continued to beat.

****

Bob Mosier didn't see the old man standing in the brush beside the road until he hollered out at the four riders. The other three evidently didn't see him either because Leroy and Mack Wade nearly shot the old coot. It could prove unwise to stand in the brush alongside a quiet road and holler at four armed men hunting someone as dangerous as Dallas Babb.

Of course, no one Bob knew praised old man Tillery for an ounce of wisdom. But men far and wide marveled at his grit. That and the fact he had only one leg. The one he didn't have, he'd left in Vicksburg back in '63.

"Damn you, Tillery, I almost put a chunk of lead in you," Wade said as he holstered his revolver. Charlie still had his Bowie knife in his hand.

"I've had lead in me before, asshole!" Tillery spat.

"Why you hollering at us anyhow?" Leroy asked.

"Cause you don't belong on this road. What are you rowdies doing down in these parts?"

"We didn't tell you?" Leroy asked.

"Hell no, you didn't tell me," Tillery said with a puzzled look.

"Well, then I don't guess it's any of your damn business, is it?" Leroy huffed.

Wade laughed at the comment. Tillery didn't. As he often did, Charlie looked confused. Bob thought it had something to do with that one crossed eye. The thoughts of gut shooting this one still tempted Bob Mosier.

"Don't you get smart mouthed with me, asshole," Tillery said to Leroy.

"What you going to do about it if I do?" Leroy asked in an amused tone of voice.

"You crawl off that hoss and put down your guns and I'll thrash your ass is what I'll do," Tillery said with conviction. He had plenty of grit.

Leroy laughed and said, "Old man, if we wasn't on urgent business I'd let Charlie here cut off your other leg. Then you'd have to slither around like a snake. You best be glad we are in a hurry."

Leroy gave his horse the spur and the other three followed after him. Old Tillery limped along behind, throwing rocks and calling them all kinds of foul names.

Bob didn't want to see any kind of harm done to the old man, him being a veteran and all, but it bothered him gravely that the four of them were seen on this road they had no business being on. It bothered Bob even more that he, of all people, might be the only one in this group of four with the good sense to know what they intended to do could lead to nothing but catastrophe.

****

Millie tugged weeds from her vegetable garden until she noticed the four riders on the horizon. The sighting raised no immediate alarm. People came and people went and besides, Millie Bardoe possessed no enemies. She gave little thought to the riders doing anything other than just keeping on riding. But when they made it up to her front yard and she recognized them, Millie grew alarmed. She knew the Mosier's and knew they were wanted for bank robbery north of there. She knew Mack Wade and the half-breed called Charlie, and knew their reputations as no goods.

Millie stood upright and wiped her hands on her apron. Leroy Mosier said something to the other three and turned his horse toward her garden. The others stayed put. Leroy didn't stop at the gate to the little picket fence, but busted through the gate and tromped his horse through her garden and right up to her.

She spoke the only words coming to mind. "Leroy Mosier, you are destroying my tomato plants."

The eldest Mosier boy donned a sickening grin and said, "Your tomato plants be damned, Missus Bardoe."

Millie fought the urge to bolt for the house. This was no time to show fear.

"What business do you have at my home, Leroy?"

"We're searching for Dallas Babb."

"Dallas is not here. Dallas has never been here," Millie said, fighting to keep her voice from betraying a consuming kind of fear.

"But we figure your husband knows the whereabouts of his nephew. And we figure if he knows, you know as well. Where is Dallas Babb?"

"My husband has no doings with his nephew." Oh how she wished her Clay were here now. If he were, these cowards wouldn't be.

"You don't want to toy with us, woman. We are prepared to do what we need to get what we came here for."

Millie now knew no option but to flee to the safety of her house. She made it around Leroy and his horse to the porch and inches from her door when one of the other men grabbed her from behind. Mack Wade wrapped his gritty arms around her waist. Millie expected to be held in place, but Wade pushed open her front door and dragged her through the threshold. All else quickly became a blur as she noticed two other figures descending upon her with hands grabbing and probing and pushing and pulling. She heard one voice of reason ring out from beyond the frenzy.

"Boys! Hey, Boys! Let's just ride out of here. Ain't no good sense in taking this any further."

The others paid the voice no mind.

They forced her to the floor. She felt the material of her day dress being ripped from her body. Millie fought, but her aggressors fought harder. One more time, she heard the lone opposing voice.

"I'll have no part of this, Leroy!"

"Well, if you won't take your turn," she heard Leroy Mosier grunt, "then you just wait outside, Bob."

One of them, and Millie didn't know which one, spread her legs, tore away her undergarments and then took her. Well before the other two did the same, Millie Bardoe lost her mind.

****

Dallas Babb felt at ease in the little shack. The abode squatted way back in the woods in a part of the county nobody would think to find him. Killing that granddaddy and his bad egg of a grandson turned out to be a stroke of luck for Babb. What had been their home now served as his hideout.

Babb wiggled in a chair while playing with his money. He liked to count it and look at it and fondle it. It practically made him giddy. He bet the old man and young boy could not have imagined in their wildest dreams this much money would one day be spread out across their table. To think he nearly bound himself to share all this with the Mosier's tended to make him feel rather foolish.

Blasting the lives out of the man and the boy delivered satisfaction, but it could not compare to the joy Babb took in shooting holes in Davy and Jake Mosier. He only regretted not getting the idea to take the money while all four of the brothers were together. But the other two would step in his path sooner or later, and he'd just kill them as easily as he did the others.

For the past couple of days when Babb felt a need to laugh, he went back and relived exactly what he said and done to the youngest Mosiers. He could play it in his mind over and over just as vividly as if it happened within the hour.

The three of them crouched around the fire.

"I sure could use some of Ma's oatmeal cookies," Davy said.

"I'd like to have one of her apple pies," Jake responded.

"I don't think my cut of the take is quite big enough, boys," Babb added to the conversation.

"What does that have to do with either cookies or pie?" Davy asked.

Babb pushed to his feet, pulled back his frock coat and took his Colt out of the shoulder holster. "Not a damned thing. But I'm a cake man."

Babb thought his own words funny and he laughed as he put two bullets in Jake Mosier's chest.

Young Davy sat there with a fully loaded Winchester across his lap, but he flung it to the ground and took off in a run like a Nancy-boy.

Babb turned his gun on the fleeing boy, cocked it and took a bead, but he didn't yet pull the trigger.

"You got to run faster than that, Davy Mosier!"

Davy looked back over his shoulder and his eyes shown as big around as silver dollar pieces. He did seem to pick up the pace.

"Get ready, Davy! I'm getting ready to pull the trigger! It's going to hurt, boy!"

Davy was a good ways gone by then, but Babb could hear him starting to cry.

He couldn't help but snicker when he pulled the trigger.

Even with hot lead in the back of his brain, Davy Mosier took three or four more running steps before toppling to the ground. He didn't move after that.

The remembered sights and sounds still worked to tickle Babb's funny muscle. Here in his newly acquired hideout he sat back, counted, looked at, and felt his money while laughing his ass off.

****

Bob Mosier slumped in the saddle and could not say why he didn't gallop away from the Bardoe house. He could hear the woman screaming and the men grunting and, at one point, Bob leaned out of the saddle and threw up what had been his morning meal. He could simply click his tongue and nudge his horse and he would be gone. Still, though, Bob sat there.

The screaming did finally stop, but the grunting continued. Bob could hear Charlie laughing.

Mack Wade came out first. He worked at buttoning his trousers with a strange expression on his face that Bob could not read. Wade didn't look at or say a single word to Bob as he swung into the saddle and trotted away.

Leroy came out a few minutes later. He wore a look on his face as indecipherable as the one Wade bore. Maybe, Bob reckoned, he'd just witnessed how men look once they surrender their souls to hell.

Leroy got on his horse and reined the dapple mare toward the road. Still, Bob sat without moving.

"What the hell are you doing? Let's get out of here," Leroy ordered.

Although Charlie remained in the house, no sounds could be heard from within.

"What about him?" Bob said with a nod toward the house.

"He ain't nothing to us, and neither is she. I'm riding. You stay if you want to."

"You did a God-awful thing here today, Leroy," Bob shouted.

Leroy turned his horse in a tight circle and moved up close to Bob. "I am revenging the death of our brothers," he snarled.

"That woman did not kill our brothers," Bob shouted again.

"Revenge is not always a simple matter," Leroy now shouted.

Bob started to dismount.

"What are you doing?" Leroy all but screamed.

"I ain't leaving her to that idiot," Bob replied.

"You don't want to go in there, Bob… " Leroy's tone caught Bob's attention.

"… as I was leaving… he started to work on her with that knife."

"Oh, dear God," Bob moaned as he settled back into his saddle.

Leroy spurred his horse to a trot. As if helpless to do anything else, Bob followed after him like he did too many times before.

The house lay not far behind them when Bob called out to his older brother.

"Clay Bardoe's revenge will surely be no simple matter."

****

Clay Bardoe sat in the small office at the back of the store recording numbers in a ledger when first the bell jingled and then a near-frantic voice bellowed his name.

"Clay! Clay Bardoe!"

Bardoe darted from the office to find Jacob Tillery just inside the doorway leaning heavily on his crutches. The elderly man gasped to catch his breath.

"I came as quickly as I could, Clay. I know them boys are up to no good," Tillery huffed.

"Calm down now, Mr. Tillery, and tell me what's going on here," Bardoe said as he moved to Tillery's side.

"I saw two of the Mosier boys, Mack Wade, and that crazy friend of his, Charlie, heading toward your place. I tried to scare them away… "

"How long ago was this, Mr. Tillery?" Bardoe interrupted.

"I came here straight away and as fast as my one leg would carry me."

"The road goes past my house," Bardoe said more for his benefit than Tillery's. "They could be on that road and not headed to my house."

Tillery began to catch his breath. "Clay, I didn't like the looks on their faces, and they were all armed to the teeth. Besides, every one of them is a criminal, and your missus is out there all by herself."

Jacob Tillery made a good point, and Bardoe no longer tried to reason away the dire possibilities. He'd done so in the first place only to save himself from a gnarling fear. In reality, he just wasted precious minutes.

Bardoe started down the street in front of his store in a dead run. He started to dodge a cowboy on a large buckskin gelding before a better option stuck in his mind.

"Mister, you name the price for your horse and the tack and I'll pay it," Bardoe shouted up to the cowboy.

"Sir, you couldn't afford what I'd demand for this here… "

"I'll pay you five hundred dollars in cash money," Bardoe butted in.

The cowboy leapt out of his saddle, pulled his rifle from the scabbard, and handed the reins to Bardoe. "Sir, you just bought everything I own in this world, except this here rifle. The horse's name is Moonshine, and I'd ask that you treat him right."

****

The form lying destroyed on his parlor room floor bore no resemblance to the woman Clay Bardoe loved more than life itself. In all actuality, the beautiful Millicent no longer occupied what remained of her body. Bardoe struggled to believe she now resided in a better place. What lie in the still spreading pool of blood could not laugh, could not tease, and therefore, could not be his Millie. Bardoe did not harbor a need to touch or comfort the remains at his feet. He might have felt otherwise if the remains still possessed a face.

Bardoe walked to the bedroom without ever feeling his feet moving beneath him. He had not in the longest time partaken of strong drink, but seemed awash in the numbing effect of too much whiskey consumed. In this state he removed a quilt from his marriage bed and draped it over the mound of desecrated and mangled flesh.

With that task accomplished, the widower Bardoe managed to put one foot after another in motion to climb the stairs to his attic. There in a chest tucked beneath the eaves, he long ago stored away the vestige of a life he once lived.

When Bardoe came down the stairs, the sound each footfall made sounded much different than they did going up the stairs. This time, ornate silver spurs jingled and the stovetop boots with the coffin toe to which they were attached pounded the wood beneath their soles. The wide black belt around his waist sported two Slim Jim holsters attached cross-draw style. Each holster bore the weight of a .45 Colt Single Action Army revolver outfitted with pearl handles. A Stetson with a Montana Peak and a "Never Flop" rim adorned his head – the brim, indeed, as stiff as the day he bought it. A calf-length duster rested in the crook of his right arm, and in his left hand he carried an 1873 Winchester.

He strode past the body of his wife without bothering to look down. Before mounting the horse named Moonshine, Bardoe put on the duster he wore last on a side street in Fort Smith. On the back of the duster directly between Bardoe's shoulder blades were three large and jagged holes.

CHAPTER FOUR

Here Are My Words

Bardoe banked on two truths. First of all, an animal can only follow its instincts, and secondly, the man known only by "Charlie" resembled in many ways a lowly animal.

Bardoe knew the exact location of the hovel Charlie called home. Because he functioned as an animal, and not a very smart one at that, Charlie would consider his hovel a safe place to flee.

Bardoe rode his new horse hard and refused to think about the beauty who had been Millicent. When those thoughts arose, he blocked them by visualizing the damage clearly done by a very large knife. He would not be there when they buried his Millie, but he would bury thoughts of the past by dwelling on the retribution he intended to impose. He could do nothing to bring back his wife. He could do everything to avenge her death. The consuming desire to do so now provided the only motivation for his heart to continue to pump his life's blood.

Bardoe galloped within a half mile of his destination before stopping to let Moonshine drink from a stream. The sun would set in another hour, and Bardoe wanted to do this deed in the broad light of day. Once Moonshine caught his breath and cooled for a bit, Bardoe mounted up and this time kept his horse at a walk.

The half-breed lived in a lean-to. Planks of cedar formed three walls leaving the front open and exposed. A clearing of no more than an acre circled the structure. Bardoe felt that the horse beneath him sensed the new master's intent, and that this fine animal, if given its reins, would have preferred to thunder in and strike like lightening. However, Bardoe held the pace to slow and deliberate.

Charlie sat on his haunches inside the lean-to preparing his evening fire. When he looked up and spotted horse and rider, Bardoe had ridden within forty yards of his prey.

Charlie stood and stepped outside his shelter, but did not run, and Bardoe did not expect him to do so.

Bardoe reined Moonshine to a halt and slowly swung out of the saddle. He pulled his rifle from the scabbard with his right hand and then brought it up and rested the barrel across his right shoulder. Thirty yards stood between him and the half-breed.

Charlie wrapped his right hand around the handle of his knife, but did not remove it from his belt. "I know why you come here!" he shouted to Bardoe.

Bardoe stood silently with the rifle across his shoulder and his left hand hanging relaxed at his side.

"You are here," Charlie shouted again, "because you want me to kill you, like I killed your woman."

A smile spread across Charlie's face, but Bardoe never changed his emotionless expression. He just stared at the man who did not have the smarts to sense his peril. Soon, however, the smile on Charlie's face dissolved into a scowl.

"Why don't you talk?"

When still he did not get a response, Charlie jerked the knife from his belt. "You say something! You say something now! I want to hear your words!"

Bardoe said nothing. And the half-breed charged. Charlie covered the distance with his knife in the air and growling like a rabid dog. Bardoe did not twitch until the very last second when he brought the Winchester off his shoulder and swung it like a club. The heavy barrel collided soundly with the side of the half-breed's head and sent him to the ground.

Charlie fell face down but rolled onto his back and never lost his grip on the knife. Bardoe stomped down on the wrist of the knife wielding hand with the heel of his boot, holding it in place. At the same time he put his rifle stock to Charlie's throat and started applying pressure. The half-breed soon gasped for air. Bardoe pushed down yet harder on the rifle and began to grind his boot heel into Charlie's wrist. The downed man tried to scream, but could only gurgle. Only seconds later his fingers unfolded from around the knife handle.

Bardoe raised his rifle and scooped up the knife. Charlie brought up the one hand he could still move and clawed at his throat while gasping for air. Bardoe calmly walked the few feet to Moonshine and slid the rifle back in its scabbard. He solemnly examined the knife in his hand for long seconds before turning back to Charlie.

Bardoe straddled the man's chest and pinned his arms to the ground with his knees. He filled his left hand with Charlie's thick black hair and jerked his head up from the ground. Bardoe shook the head viciously to arouse the nearly unconscious foe. When Charlie's eyes opened and cleared, Bardoe bent and put his mouth near Charlie's ear.

Bardoe spoke barely above a whisper. "Here are my words... I am going to send you to hell... and I'm going to do it very slowly."

Bardoe leaned back and looked down into unrepentant eyes – having no right to glare in hostility. He brought up the knife and guided it toward the disrespectful orbs.

The half-breed known only as Charlie began to scream. He screamed for the longest time. Long after he stopped, Bardoe continued to carve.

****

Bardoe felt nothing throughout the long night. No elation. No remorse. No satisfaction. For a man who never wanted to kill, his first kill came easy. The act to Bardoe seemed of little significance.

A new dawn announced its arrival on the eastern horizon and he vigilantly watched the trail from his hiding place in the timber. Other than himself, only one other human being would have reason to be on that trail.

Bardoe already had a round chambered in the Winchester

and the hammer cocked. All he had to do was wait, and watch, and pull the trigger.

****

Mack Wade spent a restless night. Nearly a pint of whiskey failed to silence the noises in his mind. Wade didn't necessarily feel bad for what he'd done to the woman. He felt bad because the woman's husband was Clay Bardoe.

Newcomers to the area would see Clay Bardoe and think, there goes a storekeeper. Those who had been around as long as Wade and who traveled in less than respectable circles, would see Clay Bardoe and think, there goes still a very dangerous man.

Wade had heard it both ways. He'd heard that Bardoe had killed a number of men, and he'd heard Bardoe never shot to kill. He didn't know the truth, but he reckoned Bardoe by now had sunk into a murderous kind of mood.

After coming to a decision on what best to do, Wade mounted up early. He spent the night a good ten miles from Charlie's place, and he wanted to be at Charlie's shortly after sunup. Then he'd try to get the breed to high-tail it down to

Texas with him. Wanted men could easily get lost in all that country.

Wade felt pretty certain Charlie wouldn't want to go. He probably would not acknowledge the danger at hand because he had too much stubborn and too little smarts. If he wouldn't go down to Texas, Wade planned to kill him. Charlie had been a decent friend, but Wade couldn't afford to leave him behind and take chances of Clay Bardoe torturing out of Charlie where Wade could be found.

Day started beating back the night and Charlie's lean-to lay just around a bend in the trail when Wade's sorrel mare grew skittish. Wade could soon enough see what his horse already sensed – something blocked the trail just a few yards ahead. From where he sat, Wade viewed what he thought to be a skinned and butchered carcass of a small white-tailed deer. When he got right up on it, he figured out real fast that it wasn't no deer.

"Good God, Charlie," Wade called down from his horse. "Someone killed you real badly."

Seeing Charlie like this set a wildfire of fear burning in Wade's guts and sent fire bells going off in his head. Wade sensed the trap. He put spur to flesh at the very moment his horse simply crumbled beneath him. Then the sound of the gunshot followed. Wade jumped free of his horse and hit the ground rolling. When he came up he'd gotten his revolver free from its holster. He started to his right in a run, but a bullet kicked up the ground in that direction. He turned to the left and a bullet tore into the earth in that direction as well. No matter which way he turned to flee, a bullet stopped his progress.

Wade never considered himself gifted with brains, but he owned enough smart to know that he wasn't going no damned place. He wanted to return fire, but he carried only so many bullets and had no idea what direction to send them flying. Mack Wade just stopped in his tracks and stood still only feet away from the bodies of his horse and only friend.

****

Bardoe stood too far away to use his pistols, but close enough to see that Mack Wade's fear showed on his face like make-up on a whore. He chambered another round in his rifle, took careful aim, and nearly blew off the hand Wade used to hold his revolver.

Wade grabbed what remained of the mangled hand with his good hand, screamed, and did a stomp dance, but didn't go down.

"Show yourself, you son of a pig!" he shouted in the wrong direction. Then in another direction he shouted, "Bardoe? That has to be you. You bastard! You've gone and ruint my gun hand!"

Bardoe took aim again and caused Wade's right foot to explode into a mist of red. This time Wade couldn't help but go down. He fell on his face, but then struggled up to his knees. He bellowed one long continuous noise that sounded half scream and half growl.

Bardoe walked back to where he'd hobbled Moonshine. In a most casual manner he put away his rifle and climbed into the saddle. He came out of the woods a few feet in front of Wade and just sat and watched the man bleed.

"You ain't gonna make this fast are you?" Wade asked with some degree of difficulty.

"Nope."

Bardoe reached with his right hand and pulled the Colt on his left side. Wade looked away as Bardoe took aim and ripped apart his other hand. For the longest time, Wade just wailed and rocked back and forth on his knees. He'd tucked the gory stumps of his hands up under his armpits. Bardoe nonchalantly put the Colt back in the long slender holster.

After a while Wade managed more words that came haltingly between grunts and groans. "I'll be durn if I ain't now wishin' that I'd listened to that cussed Bob Mosier. He tried to talk some sense into us. He wouldn't even take his turn. Just waited outside on his hoss. You might consider that when it comes his turn to face your wrath, Clay Bardoe. Now, that brother of his, Leroy? He's the one that got us in this mess. It was his damned idea to start with. When you catch up with him, tell him I hope to see him in hell!"

Bardoe climbed down from Moonshine and stepped up to stand directly in front of Wade who'd dropped his head to his chest. When he was able to look up, it was obvious by the look in his eyes what he saw for the first time.

"That's… Charlie's… knife… in your belt."

"Yup."

Bardoe pulled the knife, bent, and thrust only about four inches of it into Wade's lower guts. He gave it a little twist before pulling it back out. He intended to do just enough damage to drown Wade's insides with blood.

Wade howled like a banshee as he swayed a couple of times before toppling over on his left side. His mouth opened and closed like a fish out of water. Bardoe stooped and wiped the blade clean on Wade's shirt before sticking it back in his belt.

He mounted back up, relaxed in the saddle, and emotionlessly watched for the many minutes it took for Mack Wade to bleed out.

****

Stillwater had three undertakers, but only one who loved to gossip probably more than he loved eating. That said a lot because the undertaker, Sid Rowden, was a very fat man. There wasn't a secret in the world that could be considered safe with Sid. What Sid knew, the town would soon know.

Bardoe brought Moonshine to a stop in front of Sid Rowden's funeral parlor. The undertaker sat in a stout chair on the parlor's front porch.

"I do declare, Clay, is that two bodies you got slung and covered on that horse?" Sid asked from the porch. He didn't bother getting up. Lifting himself took a great deal of effort for Sid Rowden.

"It is in fact, Sid," Bardoe said as he dropped the lead rope he'd tied to Charlie's chestnut gelding. "I got that half-breed they called Charlie and Mack Wade under that tarp."

Bardoe sat and looked back as Sid Rowden eyed him closely for a silent and considerable moment. "Clay, you're dressed like you're marshaling again."

"I ain't marshaling, Sid."

"Did you kill them boys?"

"I certainly did, and I'll pay you to bury them. I'll also pay you to go out to my place and get my dead wife and bury her too. Put her in the cemetery next to her daddy."

Rowden hoisted his ample ass out of the chair. "Millicent's dead, Clay?" he gasped.

"She is, Sid. These two and the remaining two Mosier boys defiled her and then killed her. Charlie made a mess out of her with his knife. I'll be bringing you the Mosier boys as soon as I can. I'll also be bringing you the body of my nephew, Dallas Babb."

The undertaker clucked like a hen for several seconds before saying, "I am so sorry for your terrible loss, Clay. I'll put together a real nice service for Mill… "

"Won't be no service, Sid. Just put her in the ground."

"Will you be wanting to view Millicent once I've got her prepared, Clay?"

"I done seen her dead. Don't need to see her dead no more."

Bardoe turned Moonshine in place to face the direction from which they'd approached. "I'll be taking a room above the Drover's Saloon. I'll pay damned good money to any man or woman who can tell me the whereabouts of the Mosiers and Babb. As a matter of fact, I'll be throwing my house, land, and the general store into the mix as well. Anybody looking to find me can find me down in the saloon."

By noon tomorrow, Bardoe figured, the entire town, if not the county, would know the condition of the remains Bardoe had brought to the undertaker. That same news would find its way to both the Mosiers and Babb in no time at all.

CHAPTER FIVE

No Respectable Establishment

Bob and Leroy spent the night in a deserted shack they rode upon about fifteen miles west of Stillwater. The next morning, Bob hurriedly saddled his horse and swung into the saddle the very moment Leroy stumbled half-asleep from the shack.

"Where the hell are you going?" he asked while shading his eyes from the bright midmorning sun.

"I don't know," Bob grumbled.

"Don't know? What in tarnation do you mean you don't know?"

"I'm just riding away from you, Leroy."

Leroy scrunched his face and scratched at his matted hair. "Why would you do that?"

"I can't get that woman's screams out of mind, Leroy. I didn't even see what was being done to her. I didn't do the thing you did, and yet I can't get her screaming to leave my brain. It's making me go crazy and you... you can lay there and sleep like a baby," Bob shook his head.

"I'm riding away from you, Leroy, because I'm ashamed of you. I'm riding away from you because you are as rotten as last week's shit! And I'm no better because I did not a damned thing to stop you."

"You mean to say you ain't going to help me avenge the deaths of our brothers by tracking down Dallas Babb?"

"I'm also riding away from you, Leroy, because it has come to light in just the last two days that you are dumb as dog pecker!"

"Don't you talk to me that way, Bob, or I'll pull you from that horse and thrash you like I used to do when we was kids!"

Bob spurred his horse and popped the reins. With about twenty feet between Leroy and himself he stopped and spun his horse to face his brother.

"You and me, Leroy, are dead men, and you don't even know it. If we was to find Dallas Babb, he'd kill us both. But we don't have time to get killed by Dallas Babb because Clay Bardoe is going to hunt us down and kill us first."

"You're weak!" Leroy shouted.

"If you say I'm weak because I'm not like you, then I'm glad I'm weak," Bob said as he nudged his horse into a walk.

"Hey, Bob! I'm the only brother you got left!"

Bob looked back over his shoulder and shouted, "Yeah, and you won't be left long and neither will I!"

"We might be able to kill Bardoe if we stick together."

Bob Mosier shook his head and held nothing back. "Yeah, and you might just be even DUMBER," he yelled at his brother, "than dog pecker."

****

Sid Rowden worked faster than Bardoe thought possible, not on the bodies, but on spreading the news.

Bardoe rode from the funeral parlor to a livery and stabled Moonshine. He walked the two blocks to the Drover's Saloon and rented a room looking out over the main street. Once settled, he picked a table out downstairs in the saloon and claimed it as his headquarters. The table sat in the far back corner. It had four chairs around it, and Bardoe removed all but the one that butted up into the corner and offered an unobstructed view of the front door. He didn't plan to offer anyone a seat at his table.

The day matured to late afternoon. Three patrons stood at the bar, and bartender Rusty Gains worked behind it. Bardoe hunkered at his table in the far corner and slowly reintroduced himself to the taste of rye whiskey while keeping an eye on the entrance. He saw his sister the very second she burst through the double swinging doors. Because the Drover entertained few customers, it took her only a second or two to lock eyes with Bardoe. She covered the distance between the door and the corner table faster than a large woman with a long skirt and petticoats should find possible.

"This is no place for a lady, Lyle," Bardoe said dryly.

She pushed right up to the table and glared at her younger brother. "Are you truly going to kill Dallas?"

"If you heard that," Bardoe said as he took a sip of his whiskey, "then you heard what happened to my Millie. It seems the proper thing to do first is offer condolences."

Lyle Babb sucked in a gulp of air and pursed her lips. "I am sorry for what happened to your wife. She was a good soul and I pray that she rest in peace, but I don't know why you'd hold my Dallas responsible for her death."

Within just the last twenty-four hours Bardoe learned something new about himself – other than the fact that killing didn't really go against his grain. He learned he could sometimes say more by saying little or nothing at all. So, he didn't respond to his sister's last comment.

"He looked up to you when he was a kid and now you are going to shoot him down?"

Bardoe took another sip of whiskey.

"Why aren't you talking to me, Clay?" Lyle said shrilly.

He made her wait before finally saying, "Because you won't like what I have to say anyway. Now, goodbye, Lyle."

Lyle stomped off in a huff but turned back halfway through the saloon. "My boy is good with a gun. You taught him to be good. If you go after him, I hope it's you that dies."

Bardoe nodded, but said not a word.

****

Deputy Marshals CB Wooly and Walt Tabor stared down at the three bodies laid out in the preparation room of Sid Rowden's funeral parlor. It seemed obscene and indecent to CB that young Millicent Bardoe laid beside the very men who killed her.

In his many years of policing the Territory, Wooly saw a countless number of corpses that had died grizzly deaths. These three would go on his list at pretty near the top. Sid Rowden had done nothing to the bodies as of yet. Millicent was still in the condition Rowden found her in, and the two men had simply been pulled down from the horse and flopped on the table.

"They did awfully terrible things to her," the much younger and less experienced Walt Tabor said before having to clear his throat.

Wooly nodded his head and said, "Yeah, and my ol' pard Clay Bardoe didn't do these two any favors either."

Earlier in the day the two deputy marshals rode out of town after finding no clues to lead them to either Dallas Babb or the remaining Mosiers. But as they headed back to Guthrie and only a short distance out of town, the Stillwater town marshal, Gray Wilson, caught up with them.

"I need you boys back in Stillwater. I got a humdinger on my hands and I want it off."

Gray explained all he learned from the undertaker Rowden.

"Have you went and talked to Clay?" Wooly asked.

"I've never had a problem admitting to no man that I ain't Wyatt Earp or Bat Masterson. To tell you boys the truth, I'd turn this here badge in before going into the Drover Saloon and challenging Clay Bardoe with what did and did not happen. From what I've seen, the man is already in a very foul mood. Besides, none of the killin' took place in the city limits. This ain't my jurisdiction. It ain't my job. It belongs to you boys."

"It all happened in Payne County," Wooly pointed out. "Let the sheriff handle it."

"No sir, he don't want it either. We done talked and we'd like the judge in Guthrie to investigate and handle this as a federal matter. Like I said, it belongs to you boys."

Standing over the bodies now, Wooly shook his head and summed it all up, "Lord, Lord, Lord."

"How we going to handle this, CB?" Tabor asked.

"Like a rattlesnake," Wooly mumbled.

They were leaving Rowden's establishment when Marshal Gray Wilson approached them a second time. "Deputy Wooly, I was over at the telegraph office when this came in for you."

Wooly opened the telegraph, read it to himself, and then could only sigh long and hard.

"Trouble?" Tabor asked.

"My old mama's died back in Virginia. I don't know that this day could get any worse."

****

The Drover's saloon conducted a brisk evening business as Bardoe watched CB Wooly and Walt Tabor walk in and look around until they spotted him.

Wooly strolled right up to the table, but Tabor hung back a couple of paces. Bardoe had his two Colts displayed on the table top with a bottle of whiskey and a shot glass. Wooly looked down at the pistols and then looked around for a chair. They'd been removed and he clearly got the message.

"Howdy, Clay."

"Howdy, CB."

Tabor spoke out, "Hello, Mr. Bardoe."

Bardoe glanced at the young deputy and acknowledged him with a nod.

"Your life's taken a hard and sharp twist, ain't it, old friend?" CB asked.

"That it has."

"I offer my deepest apologies and regrets over the loss of your precious wife, Clay."

"Thank you, CB."

"I got news my mama died yesterday back in Virginia," Wooly said more to himself than to Bardoe.

"I'm sorry to hear that, CB," Bardoe said with the deepest sincerity. "It's tough on a man when his mama dies."

"Well, she was old. I guess I'll be headed back on a train tomorrow."

"I wish you safe passage, CB."

Wooly took a deep breath and nodded his head a few times before plunging on.

"Not much has changed around here in the Oklahoma and Indian Territories, Clay. It's always been mostly a calamitous breed who settles here."

Bardoe shook his head in response. "There you'd be wrong, CB. It's mostly a vicious and murderous breed that settles here."

"Well, I can't honestly argue that point, but I can say this… you've never been the vicious and murderous type, but you went plumb savage on those two ol' boys, Clay."

"That I did. Did you see my Millie?"

"I did."

"Could you help but notice the bite marks on her neck and shoulders? I bet there was some on her teats too before Charlie cut them off and chopped them up."

Wooly rubbed at his face and eyes before saying more. "The local law is going to ask the federal judge to take this case. I don't know what direction that may go off on. But I'd ask you, Clay... no, I'll beg you... please don't take the law any further into your own hands. Please, let the others be."

"CB, that judge will have to do what he has to do. Then you will have to do what you have to do. And meanwhile, I will be doing what I have to do. I'll be trying to find and kill Leroy Mosier, Bob Mosier, and Dallas Babb. And I do not intend for their dying to be either fast or pretty."

"Well, Clay," Wooly exhaled, "you are right in that a man has to do what a man has to do. By and by, I would ask you to consider this. You have been known in life as Deputy Marshal Bardoe, and store owner Bardoe, and husband Bardoe. Don't cast a shadow on those honors by being last known as killing Bardoe."

Bardoe offered no response. A long period of silence followed.

"Clay," Wooly finally said, "this is no respectable establishment."

"You are right about that, CB. But it is the type of place that the kinds of people I'm looking for frequent. There will be those passing through here who know where I can find the Mosiers and Babb."

CB Wooly's shoulders slumped. "Clay, I don't want to have to come after you with a warrant."

Bardoe considered taking a swig of whiskey, but felt past the point where that would be a good idea. "CB, let it be known," Bardoe said solemnly, "that I will kill *any man* that comes between me and those that destroyed my life."

CB Wooly adjusted the Boss of the Plains hat on his head and said, "I'm sorry it's come to this, Clay."

"No sorrier than I," Clay mumbled. Then he took a swig.

Wooly turned and walked away. He strode several paces before glancing back to observe Walt Tabor backing out of the saloon with his eyes glued on Bardoe and a hand real damned close to his holstered revolver. Wooly spun on his partner.

"Walt, never fear turning your back on Clay Bardoe. If he chooses to put a bullet in you, he'll do it while looking you in the eye."

CHAPTER SIX

Liquor and Lovin'

Leroy Mosier spent the rest of the day and that night at the deserted old shack. By the next morning he ran out of both food and whiskey. He would bet just about anything that his brother Bob would have shown back up well before now. Maybe ol' Bob had been serious. Leroy had no other choice than to ride off without him. He damned sure wasn't going to sit here and starve or go a day without whiskey.

A second cousin on his ma's side named Ray Potts lived a little over ten miles away. He'd not only be good for a meal, but Cousin Ray always kept a jug or three cooling in his root cellar. After a couple of days or so of laying low, and eating well, and drinking even better, Leroy could ride out to find Mack Wade and Charlie.

Leroy took plenty of time to think it all out. The way he saw it, Bob was spooked because he tended to believe any and every darned thing he heard. Leroy heard it all too – how Clay Bardoe had been the greatest shootist to ever pin on a Deputy United States Marshal badge – that he was rough and tough, and calm as a mud puddle under gun fire. Sure, Leroy had heard it all, but Leroy understood things Bob didn't. Things such as, people love to pass on legends and legends tend to grow with each and every telling. Chances were most of the talk about Clay Bardoe had been exactly that – talk.

Besides, Leroy asked himself, could a man of those supposed skills and temperament truly lower himself to run a general store? Leroy couldn't see how. Only one fact remained in this entire mess that Leroy knew to be absolute – Dallas Babb killed his brothers and now had his money. Leroy planned on gathering up Wade and Charlie and getting that money, and probably finding out in the process that Babb, like his uncle, earned his reputation as a result of a whole lot of talking.

The beautiful morning made for a pleasant ride and Leroy covered the ten miles in good time. His stomach growled like a thunder storm as his cousin's place came into view. A passel of barking and baying hounds signaled Leroy's arrival and brought Ray Potts out of the house.

"How you do, Cousin Ray?" Leroy called with a grin as he pulled his right boot from the stirrup and started to dismount.

"You just stay up there on that horse, Cousin Leroy," Potts called back.

Leroy eased back into the saddle with a mighty confused feeling. Ray had always been the friendly sort. Especially to kinfolk.

"Cousin Ray, is something the matter?"

"Clay Bardoe's the matter. Hell, Cousin, he's out to find you and do you up as badly as he did them other two boys. I can't have you seen around my place. I don't want no trouble with that man."

"What are you babbling about?" Leroy asked with a furrowed brow.

"Now don't be trying to play me for a fool, Leroy Mosier. It's all around town what you boys did to Clay Bar…"

"I know that part, Cousin. Are you saying he's already got to a couple of my partners?"

"Got to? Hell, Ray, he killed them deader than a tree stump. I hear…"

"Which ones, Ray? Who did he kill?"

Ray Potts scratched a balding head. "I don't remember no names, but..."

"My brother Bob Mosier... was he one of them?"

"Your brother's my cousin. Hell, I'd remember that name. You think I'm stupid in the head or something?"

Leroy's stomach had knotted up like a tyke's shoe string. Now, he exhaled a sigh of relief, but the news still held anything but good. "Mack Wade and Charlie, are you sure they're dead?"

"That's the big news in Stillwater, Cousin Leroy. John Derry from down the road a piece? He was in town yesterday and went to see the bodies. But you're right. Those are the names now that I heard them again, Mack Wade and Charlie... I don't remember his last name."

"Ain't got one," Leroy mumbled as his mood turned black as night. "How'd he kill them?"

"That's what makes it news. On that Charlie, Bardoe used the man's own knife to cut off every body part that can be removed. Derry says he heard it from the undertaker that he also gutted him like a fish and popped out his eyeballs. That other man... Wade? The word is Bardoe shot him several times in places to just make him hurt, and then belly stabbed him to ensure he'd go slow and ugly."

The realization smacked Leroy like a fist upside the face. Bob was right. It wasn't just talk about the kind of man they'd done terribly wrong.

"Cousin Leroy, you're looking all peaked, and I can't blame you. It's just a matter of time until he gets you and Bob, too. I'm sorry and I don't mean to be unsociable like, but you can understand how I can't have you coming..."

Cousin Ray Potts babbled on while Leroy turned his horse and took off in a trot. If he'd had anything in his stomach, he'd have lost it.

****

The bartender Rusty Gains could pick them out the minute they came through the front doors. They stood out like a dog turd on a kitchen table top. The Drover's Saloon never endured their types before, but in the last two days they'd been coming in from Arkansas, Kansas, Missouri, and a few even came up from Texas. Gains caught this one's attention and waved him over to the bar.

"I'm looking for... " the prissily dressed man in the short bowler began.

"I know who you're looking for," Gains cut him off, "but you don't want to find him."

"I beg your pardon?"

"Look back behind you at that table in the corner. See that man staring at you?"

"The brim of his hat is pulled too low. I can't see his eyes."

"You don't want to," Gains grinned. "But you can see those two pistols and that huge – assed knife laid out on the table, can't you?"

"I certainly can. The sight sends an ominous signal."

"That it does. Heed the warning."

"I beg your pardon?" The reporter asked once again.

"Mr. Bardoe commented this morning that he will tell his story to no more reporters. He swore not an hour ago that he would shoot between the legs the very next newspaper man that approached his table."

"Do you believe he is serious?"

"Only one way to find out."

The dapper reporter sighed hard and suddenly looked all kinds of perplexed. "But I have ridden so far."

"Do you want to be able to ride back?"

Mere seconds later, the reporter, like the previous three before him, skedaddled. Mr. Bardoe had told Gains that the reporters were starting to get in his way of doing business. Bardoe also said he figured he'd by now put out in enough directions, through enough newspapers, the bait necessary to attract his nephew, Dallas Babb.

With this last reporter scurrying back out the way he came, Gains looked to the rear corner table and nodded and smiled as Clay Bardoe showed his appreciation with a tug at his razor sharp hat brim.

****

Bob Mosier rode up to the cabin he was born in to find his dear old mother standing on the porch holding a shotgun across her chest.

Her deeply lined face looked every bit as sad and tired as it had been the day she stood watch over Davy and Jake. She brought the long barrel of the old single shot down and pointed it directly at Bob.

Bob grew confounded and spoke the first words coming to mind. "Ma, do you intend to shoot me?"

"Your pa's brother rode in from Stillwater yesterday. He told us what you boys did to that poor woman. I can't no longer lay eyes on you or Leroy."

"Ma, I didn't take any part in that abomination, but that's rightly the reason I'm here now. I told them to stop, but they didn't. I should have done more, but I didn't. Now, the sounds of how she screamed just won't let me be. Ma, I rode away from that house and left that woman to the evil hands of that half-breed Indian, Charlie. I've decided I need to ride against that man and kill him dead to silence the screams I'm still hearing."

Bob removed his hat. "I'm here now, Ma, to tell you and Pa so long. Chances are good Charlie will best me, or Bardoe will catch me coming or going."

Ma lowered her shotgun and slowly started shaking her head. "Boy, don't you know? Clay Bardoe already caught up with and did awful things to both Charlie and that Wade man. They are both dead and burnin' in hell."

Bob couldn't help his mouth from falling open or his face from flushing in fear. "I reckon I won't be far behind them," he mumbled.

Ma Mosier propped her shotgun up next to the front door. "Son, you didn't touch that woman? You didn't defile her?"

"No, ma'am. I swear on the souls of Davy and Jake that I didn't even go in that house."

Ma Mosier nodded her belief, and it looked to Bob that a tiny bit of the sad on her face dwindled away.

"Bob, you need to find a place to stay out in the woods during the day. You can come home after sundown. It would be best if you leave out every morning before the sun comes up. I'll try to hide you from Clay Bardoe the best I know how."

Bob sat and nodded his head several times, but pondered another matter. "Ma? How will I now stop hearing those screams?"

"Boy, you'll most likely hear them screams 'til the day you die."

****

Dallas Babb rode well north of the Kansas state line. The night before, while still in the dead granddaddy's shack, he awakened a little past midnight feeling he'd laid low long enough. The time came to do more with all that money than just play with it. He headed to Wichita to live the good life. If he spent up all the money he now had, Wichita owned plenty of banks just ripe for picking. He'd hit one, or maybe two, and head off for some other glorious city.

Throughout the day Babb passed fellow travelers both coming and going. None paid him any mind, and he hadn't seen any he cared to pass the time of day with, until now. Just ahead and coming his way traveled a man mounted on a grand white horse, and the man exhibited a prosperous figure. He sported a Prince Albert frock coat and a fancy brocaded vest. He wore around his waist a silk sash from which protruded the handles of two big revolvers. A large brimmed hat with a high and impressive crown perched at a jaunty angle upon the man's head. It occurred to Babb at that very moment that this form of dress would fit a man of his means in route to a refined city like Wichita.

"Excuse me, sir," Babb said with his most fetching smile, "I can't help but notice that fine white horse and your dandy apparel!" Dallas Babb possessed the ability to charm when charming became necessary.

"Why, thank you, lad," the stranger said with an air of arrogance.

"Tell me, sir, is there a place between here and Wichita that I could outfit myself in such a manner? You can't tell by looking, but I, too, am a man of some wealth."

"No, son," the man replied, "but once you reach Wichita you can buy just about anything your purse can afford."

Babb pointed at the man's pistols. "Those are impressive pieces, but your sash prevents me from making clear identification. What are you packing?"

"These are .36-caliber Colt 1851 Navy revolvers. The same iron preferred by the late Wild Bill Hickok," the dandy beamed.

Babb shook his head in appreciation and then came to the point. "Sir, how much, here and now, would it take for me to buy your horse, clothes, and those revolvers?"

The expression on the traveler's face sobered. "Why, Mister, nothing I have is for sale. Besides, what would I wear and what would I ride?"

"Why hell, man," Babb chuckled, "you'd wear my clothes and ride this here horse."

The man straightened in his saddle. "Young man, you must be touched in the head. I ask that you clear my path so that I might proceed."

Babb tugged on his reins and yielded the way. He let the man and his horse travel the distance of a good forty paces before hollering out to get his attention.

"Sir, I am not so easily dissuaded."

The man wheeled the white horse to face Babb. "Are you persisting in an attempt to annoy me?" he called back.

"I tried to do the right thing. I tried to buy what I wanted. Now, I'm forced to take it," Babb said with a relaxed grin before adding a final suggestion. "This would be the time to go for your guns."

The man made the mistake of simply cocking his head and looking at Babb like he might be a common type of idiot. Dallas Babb pulled the .41 Colt from his shoulder holster and put a bullet square dab between the dandy's eyes.

Babb stopped at a stream a few miles further north to wash the blood from the dead man's boiled white shirt front and the collar of the Prince Albert frock coat. It would prove a small price to pay for the grand appearance he'd make riding into Wichita.

****

Leroy Mosier rode with his head down and shoulders slumped. He already considered all options and found all wanting. There remained only one certainty. He did not intend to hide out in the woods and live like an animal. In the last couple of miles he'd drawn the conclusion that Bardoe would sooner or later find him and do hideous things to his body until he was cold-ass dead. This being the case, why live in misery under the elements, when Bardoe could just as easily torture him to death in a more comfortable surrounding?

Leroy had just enough money on him for a bottle of whiskey and a night tangled in the sheets with a soiled dove. He considered striking out for towns further in the distance, but thought what a pity it would be for Bardoe to catch up with him on the road and deprive him of the opportunity for liquor and lovin'.

If someone he knew saw him headed in the direction he now headed, that person would question whether or not Leroy possessed a lick of sense. That person might even think him daft, but Leroy could give a damn what any man or woman now said or thought of him because he'd soon be dead anyway.

The town of Stillwater sat nearly five miles straight in front of his horse's nose. If he got lucky, Leroy might sneak through the town and into Miss Laura's house and buy some of her whiskey and one of her girls. If he didn't get lucky, Bardoe would get to him first.

CHAPTER SEVEN

Tit for Tat

Late in the evening Bardoe sat sharpening the knife when the madam Laura Campbell strolled into the Drover's and directly to his table.

Bardoe put down the Bowie to tip his hat. "Evening, Miss Laura."

"Evening, Mr. Bardoe."

Bardoe stared at the woman and waited for her to explain her business at his table. The madam stared down at the big knife.

When she finally looked up, she cocked her head and replied, "I find it strange that a man would keep on his person the very knife used to kill his wife."

"I find it strange," Bardoe deadpanned, "that a woman in your profession would find anything strange."

"Ah, tit for tat, Mr. Bardoe," Laura said with an appreciative smile.

"Why are you here?" Bardoe asked.

"My, but you do get right to the point."

Bardoe picked the knife back up and again applied the whetstone. He would bet a woman used to having attention would not do well without it. It took only seconds of his silent indifference to bring her to the point as well.

"I can give you Leroy Mosier. What are you willing to pay?"

Bardoe felt his heartbeat quicken. He dropped the stone into a vest pocket and slipped the knife into his belt. "I hope you are not toying with me."

"Mr. Bardoe, I am a very busy and smart woman. I have too little time and too much plain old common sense to toy with you."

Bardoe glared at the madam for long seconds before slowly nodding his belief in her credibility. "I have a house on a hundred and sixty acres. The house and eighty acres will go to the person who leads me to Leroy Mosier. The other eighty acres goes for Bob Mosier."

Laura Campbell leaned down close. "Leroy is in room 12 of my house. It's upstairs, second door on the right."

****

Deputy United States Marshal Walt Tabor stood in the shadows across from the Drover's Saloon. He knew which window looked out from the room Clay Bardoe rented. He waited for the gas light to be lit and then extinguished, signaling Bardoe was in for the night and that Tabor could also retire for a few hours of rest.

Tabor expected Bardoe to go to bed. Instead, Bardoe suddenly stepped out onto the sidewalk, turned left and strode away as if in pursuit of something... *or someone...* of significance. Tabor hung back, stayed in the shadows, and kept Bardoe in view. His heart already raced, but when it became apparent Bardoe's destination was Madam Laura's house of prostitution, Tabor's heart felt as if it would come up through his throat. Clay Bardoe could not be so all-fire fixed for just an hour or so with a whore. Tabor picked up his pace to a near run. He entered the front door of the establishment only moments behind Bardoe.

Bardoe had already reached the foot of the staircase and began taking the steps two at a time. Tabor got a clear view of the three holes in the back of Bardoe's duster, and a chill tickled at his spine. The thought did cross Tabor's mind to simply add a fourth hole, but back shooting a man without first issuing a proper warning didn't set right with the deputy.

"Mr. Bardoe!" Tabor called out.

****

Clay Bardoe did not immediately recognize the voice, but it brought him to a standstill because it sounded the two words – simply a title and his name – in a demandingly urgent manner. He slowly turned to face the distraction.

Walt Tabor stood just inside the door.

"I don't think you truly want to be here, Deputy," Bardoe said.

"Not especially," Tabor agreed, "but I reckon that one of the Mosier boys or even Dallas Babb is at the top of those stairs, and I have a warrant for any one or all three of them. You are interfering, Mr. Bardoe, with the business of the United States government."

"And you, sir, are interfering with mine," Bardoe growled.

"I don't intend to let you take the law into your own hands," Tabor said with conviction.

Bardoe drew in a deep breath and forced himself to take moments that might spare this young man's life. "Leroy Mosier is up there. He's the one that planned and led the raid against my home. Hanging will not repay his debt, and spending the rest of his life in prison damned sure won't do it. I will be going up there now to give him what he truly deserves. I won't let any force stand in my way."

Bardoe started back up the stairs.

"Clay Bardoe," Tabor called after him, "you can consider this a final warning!"

Bardoe stopped and turned once more to face the lawman.

"You just went one warning too far," Bardoe said calmly as he pushed his hat back on his head. His next words held more of an edge.

"Take your gun out, point it at me, and cock the hammer."

Tabor suddenly sprouted the expression of a man who did not understand what he was hearing.

"DO IT NOW, BOY!" Bardoe's shout sounded with the intensity of a thunder clap in the cavernous lobby.

Some of the girls and their patrons sitting about in the lobby grew engrossed in the exchange up to this point. Bardoe's booming demand now served two purposes. The onlookers scurried out of the line of fire, and Deputy Tabor did exactly as ordered.

Bardoe could now lower his voice to the typical calm and ice-cold manner he found most effective in these situations. "I'm giving you the first shot. If I'm still standing after that shot, I am going to pull one or both of my Colts and shoot you various times in the head and face."

"Mr. Bardoe, I don't want... "

"You are wasting my time. You have five seconds to pull that trigger."

"But, Mr. Bardoe, this is not... "

"You now have four... three... two... "

The deputy marshal tossed his revolver to the floor out in front of him. He dropped his head for a number of seconds before removing his badge and flinging it to join his gun. Having rendered his resignation, Walt Tabor turned and shuffled out of Miss Laura's house of ill repute.

****

She wasn't the prettiest girl in the Territory, but she was a far shot from being the ugliest. She smelled good, too. Not all whores did. Not even the slightest stink of a rotten tooth existed on this one. So, Leroy could not hold her responsible for the problem at hand.

Even though Leroy gulped a good third of his bottle before they went up to the room, it had still been okay at first. Everything worked fine and dandy just like nature intended it to. But then the girl, named Jenny, noticed the infected wound on Leroy's right shoulder.

"Why, honey," Jenny giggled, "that's a bite mark. Your last girl must have been a feisty one!"

The malfunction did not result at the thought of the Bardoe woman or even what Leroy had done or caused to be done to her. The blame lay with the thought of what the woman's husband intended for Leroy. The fear of what lie ahead made Leroy fall limp.

Now because he couldn't have the woman, he drank heavily from his bottle. The girl Jenny lay silently beside him. Nothing had been said since he rolled off her in defeat.

"You don't know it," Leroy broke the silence, "but you are lying with a dead man."

The girl said nothing and soon snored lightly. Leroy started to nod off as well.

At first he thought it a dream when the door to room 12 swung open and banged against the wall.

****

Bardoe stomped across the planked floor and wrapped his hands around Leroy Mosier's neck. He jerked the tall man forward in the bed so he could choke him and bang his head on the headboard at the same time. Leroy's arms flailed and his legs kicked, but mere seconds of having his wind cut off and his head bashed against wood, took the fight out of him. He offered no resistance when Bardoe switched from choking and banging to furiously pounding his face with both fists.

The whore lying next to Leroy rolled off the side of the bed and scampered on her hands and knees to the far wall. Bardoe did not turn from his onslaught to pay her any mind. He had in his hands the man wholly responsible for his wife's gruesome death. Had Leroy Mosier not concocted the idea and then led his gang to Bardoe's home, none of this would now be happening. This truth fueled the terrible beating that Bardoe considered far from being finished.

When Bardoe grew winded from punching and his arms started to tire, he grabbed Mosier by the bloody and matted hair of his head and rolled him out of the bed. Leroy hit the floor like a bag of potatoes and let out a tortured moan.

Bardoe heard it only as an annoyance coming from the same mouth that issued the edict that led to Millie's horror. No mouth ever deserved being silenced more than this one.

Bardoe began to stomp on Mosier's already damaged head with the two inch heels of his calfskin boots. In no time at all the boots were soaked in blood and Leroy Mosier lay unrecognizable. What little life remained in him after hitting the plank floor was now thoroughly stomped asunder. That didn't stop Bardoe from starting to kick at the midsection of the lifeless body. What did finally stop him were the familiar four clicks of a Colt being cocked.

The whore trembled in the far corner and had Mosier's gun pointed at Bardoe.

"Put the gun down, woman," Bardoe said in a mild tone.

"You're a bad man, and you deserve to die!"

"I don't disagree with you, and if this was the last man I had to kill, I'd gladly take a bullet. Currently, though, I can't let you kill me. Throw the gun away."

Instead the girl pulled the trigger and the bullet smacked the wall right above Bardoe's head. Without hesitating she thumbed back the hammer again.

Bardoe pulled the Colt on his left with his right hand and then the whore was dead. It didn't occur to him until she fell that he could have aimed to wound. As he turned to leave, he noticed the bottle on the bedside table still containing two good swallows. Bardoe picked it up, swigged the contents and then viscously threw the empty bottle against the far wall. Shattered remnants rained down on the young girl's dead body.

Bardoe made his way back to the Drover's Saloon. With every step he cursed what little remained of both Leroy Mosier and the man who Millicent Bardoe had loved.

CHAPTER EIGHT

Oh, Hell Fire

B ob Mosier stood way back in the woods earlier in the day and watched the procession of a few caring souls following the hearse up to the Mosier cabin. He observed his elderly mother step out of the cabin and collapse, and he stood idly by as his old pa helped the very fat undertaker and a few other men lift the coffin from the back of the hearse. He saw them open the coffin, and he winced as some recoiled in horror. Two of the women helped his mother from the ground and up to the pine box. From his hiding place way back in the woods he could hear her gut wrenching screams of agony.

He wanted to go down and help his pa and the other men dig the grave, but he didn't. He wanted to mount up and ride like hell for Stillwater and confront the man who delivered this nightmare to his undeserving parents, but he didn't. Bob didn't have the gumption to do either. If he went down to help, the news would get back to Bardoe of his whereabouts, and Bardoe would run him down and kill him. If he went to confront the man, Bardoe would kill him.

The remaining Mosier boy did, for the rest of the day, the only thing he could do. He hid in the woods like the coward he knew himself to be. When he wasn't crying, he prayed. He prayed for his ma and his pa. He prayed for his dead brothers, and he prayed for Missus Bardoe. He couldn't bring himself to pray for either himself or Clay Bardoe. God would only curse him further for doing so. More than once during the seemingly endless day, he considered throwing his lariat over a branch and robbing Bardoe of ending his torment.

Bob Mosier rode his horse down to the cabin under the cover of darkness. A glow from lamps could be seen radiating from the windows. After tending his horse, he removed his hat and stepped through the front door.

His ma and pa slumped in chairs at the table. Ma had long since cried herself out. Pa looked much older than the last time Bob paid him any attention.

"They brought your last brother back today," Ma said.

"I saw them," Bob mumbled.

"I couldn't even tell he'd been one of mine," she sighed. "Bardoe pounded him to pulp using nothing else but his hands and boots."

Mosier dropped his head to stare at the floor. He spent a considerable length of time up in the woods wondering what God-awful means Bardoe harnessed to kill his brother. Mosier considered about every kind of killing means except Bardoe savagely using his bare hands. A man so good with a gun, and now owning a most horrible knife, would have to surely be in a murderous frenzy to bloody his hands in such a personal manner.

Bardoe butchered Charlie, shot Wade to pieces, and pummeled Leroy. Being the last one standing who had ridden on the Bardoe house, Bob could be certain that as badly as the others died, Bardoe had something most horrendous in mind for him. So many possibilities flooded Bob's mind that his knees nearly buckled on him right there in front of his ma and pa. He might have fainted right away like a sissified school boy had his father not gotten his attention and diverted his unhealthy thinking.

Pa tried to push up from the table but struggled with the simple task. Bob couldn't ever recall seeing the tough old man show any kind of pain, and he certainly never heard him groaning like this.

"Pa?"

"Got to get to bed," was the father's only response.

"Pa, are you ailing?"

Ma stood and lent a hand to help her man. "He ain't ailing," she sighed. "He's just dug one too many graves in too short a time."

Bob headed to bed as well, but sleep wanted nothing to do with him. This night, after having watched his mother's reaction to seeing Leroy in the coffin, he had another woman's screams to listen to in his mind. Bob lay in the bed thinking of the screams, wondering how much time he had left, and how Bardoe would deal with him.

When he knew for sure he'd spend the night struggling with the thoughts, he got up and went out into the dark and straight to the barn. He came out with a shovel and walked the few hundred feet to the line of three long mounds of dirt each separated by five feet of ground. Bob paced off five feet from the third mound and started digging.

****

Martha Henry owned and ran the Peacock Saloon and Hotel in Wichita, Kansas. Late evening business boomed as the tall, young, and good looking gentleman entered her establishment. Martha watched a lot of men come and a lot of men go, but few had grabbed her attention like this one.

Another woman of her age might not possess the confidence to entertain thoughts of a liaison with a man numerous years younger in age. However, Martha knew from much experience that as long as the water they sipped tasted sweet, the age of the well from whence it came mattered little to young men. On her part, a younger man tended to more frequently scratch her incessant itch.

Martha laid aside the paper she perused. Her passion for getting "scratched" proved only slightly more demanding than her passion for staying abreast of news in Wichita and the surrounding areas. It benefited her business to know who was who, and who was doing what. Both the notorious and the infamous often visited the Peacock.

Martha beat a path straight toward the stranger. If she didn't do it, one of her girls would. The closer she drew, the more Martha believed she would not be sorry for her blatant aggression. This young man, sporting the Prince Charles frock coat would, Martha was convinced, turn out to be a man she would want to know. Using the waist sash to hold his two magnificent pistols served as a designation of both class and daring.

"Good evening, sir, and welcome to the Peacock," Martha said, offering her hand. "I am the proprietor, Martha Henry."

The boy took her hand but didn't seem certain what to do with it. "Hello, ma'am," he nodded. "My name is Bob Smith."

Martha could not help but smile at the obvious alias and a lie for which she took no offense. A young man was most always fine. A young and mysterious man... well... my, my. She could also not help but notice a glaring sign that this lad was on the lam. While on the run, he'd clearly lost weight. The magnificent suit of clothes were a tad too large for him.

The fact that this man was wanted did nothing for Martha but contribute to her want as well. Martha Henry always held in her heart... and loins... a special place for naughty boys.

"Are you here just for the evening, Mister... Smith? Or, will you be needing a room?" Martha asked as she moved close enough to press her famed cleavage snugly against the handsome stranger's chest.

Martha found it most delightful when he grinned like a

school boy, and said in a near whooping fashion, "Why, hell, I hope I'm going to need a room!"

****

CB Wooly's grand ancestral home presently belonged solely to him. He knew it one day would, and he planned all along to sell the house and land, along with all the furnishings. Now, as Wooly sat alone in the dark parlor during the wee hours of the morning, he considered options other than selling.

Wooly bore a heavy heart, not solely for the fact that he had just the previous day put his mother in the ground next to the much older graves of his father and two older brothers, who both died fighting for Robert E. Lee.

In just a few short hours, he'd catch a train that would carry him back to the Oklahoma and Indian Territories – the country he'd called home for so long, and the place he thought he'd never give up for this house and land, in his native state of Virginia. Now, Wooly had found a very good reason to stay in Virginia and forsake both the country and job that meant so very much to him.

During the short time he'd been away, CB had no contact with anyone back west. He had no confirmation that the situation in Stillwater had grown only worse, but he knew all too well Clay Bardoe. Clay would no doubt conduct the business of avenging his wife's death in the same manner he once conducted the business of tracking down and arresting outlaws. The Clay Bardoe Wooly knew could boast of many a favorable attributes – tenacity topping the list. He had never known the man to quit or back down. Wooly felt certain Bardoe had shed more blood in his absence, and that warrants for his arrest would be forthcoming. Federal judges did not tolerate vigilantism in the west for fears of it spreading like a plague.

Wooly now had to decide whether or not he measured up to the task of going back and trying to serve those warrants on a once close friend and now a very dangerous man. Wooly could stay in his ancestral estate and live to be a very old southern gentleman, or he could go back to the place and life that fit him like a glove. The place he was most likely not live to see another Christmas.

****

Bob Mosier squatted on a log watching the small fire he built to make some coffee. Ma had been packing him away with food to last throughout the day. He munched on a cornbread muffin while the flames had him thinking of hell, and wondering if hell awaited him. Robbing that bank had been the worst sin committed his whole life long. It didn't seem right for a man to burn forever over something like that.

Bob crammed the last of the muffin in his mouth and reached for the coffee pot when the snapping sound of foliage came from behind him but not in the direction of his hobbled horse. Without bothering to turn and look, Bob went from bending to an all-out run. He pumped his arms and stretched his legs for all his worth before it dawned on him that there was no sound of someone crashing through the timber after him. Bob stopped and listened. He did hear leaves, sticks and brush being trampled, but the faint sound signaled someone moving in the opposite direction.

"Oh, hell fire!" he exclaimed as he took off in another dead run, but this time back from where he'd come. Someone had obviously spotted him and was trying to make a getaway. Bob ran with the speed and determination of a man who stood to die in a nasty manner if he didn't catch the other man. He soon caught a glimpse of a blue cotton work shirt and a mop of frizzy hair. Bob closed in on his prey. He didn't know at what point, but he'd pulled his pistol and looked for an opportunity to pull the trigger as well. He caught up enough to see the man wore bibbed overalls, with only one shoulder strap snapped. The other flopped out behind him like an offset tail. The man was also in his bare feet, but Bob didn't notice that until the man leapt in the air to clear a downed tree, and didn't make it. He rolled about on the ground and held onto the foot he snagged while Bob ran to him and thrust his revolver down and into a very young face.

"Damn! How old are you, boy?"

"I'm fifteen, Mr. Mosier!"

"Damn! You know who I am?"

"Yes, sir. You're Bob Mosier."

"Damn!"

"That bank up in Ponca, and Mr. Bardoe too, is offering a lot of money for anyone who knows where you can be found."

"And now you know, don't you, boy?" Bob exhaled in a moan.

"Yes, sir, I do."

"And do you know boy that I am now going to have to kill you?" Bob groaned.

"I don't want to die, Mr. Mosier!"

"And I don't want to kill you, son!"

For several seconds the boy rubbed his foot as Bob pointed his gun but neither said a word.

"If I let you go," Bob finally said, "will you promise not to turn me in?"

"It's just me and my ma, Mr. Mosier. We need that money in a bad kind of way. I won't lie to you. You let me be, and I still have to tell what I know."

"Boy… I wish you'd lied to me," Mosier said as he thumbed back the hammer.

Tears welled in the kid's eyes, but he didn't beg. "I just ain't no liar."

Mosier put the barrel down close to the boy's head and then jerked it up and away. "Yeah, and I ain't no killer. Get out of here boy. And I hope you know what you're about to do is going to get me dead."

It was no consolation that the boy did have a pained look on his face as he hobbled off in a half run on his hurting foot. He hadn't made it far when Bob Mosier called after him.

"Ain't really your fault boy that I'm going to be dead. I pretty much brought that on my own self."

****

Dallas Babb awoke to find Martha Henry standing beside her bed and already fully dressed.

"What time is it?" he yawned.

"It's early yet, darling, but I'm an early riser. I do love my morning paper and coffee. You just stay here and I'll send up some of the help with your breakfast in an hour or so."

Martha had brought Babb up to her wondrous and finely furnished room. He never before knew such splendor, either in a room nor a woman. Dallas Babb would not soon forget the night before – no it was a night he would never forget. From the glow on the lady's face and the smile she beamed, he felt certain, she too might be a while in forgetting the role he played in their merriment.

Martha left and Babb dozed. An old woman brought up breakfast; Babb ate it, and then dozed some more. Shortly before lunch, he dressed and went downstairs to greet the day along with the magnificent owner of the Peacock Saloon and Hotel. After last evening's brief acquaintance, fornication, and free bed and board, only a fool would not dread that a hand-shake and a fare-thee-well might be all Martha Henry would contribute on this day.

The moment Babb spotted and made eye contact with Martha, it became apparent that he had no need for unease. She looked as delighted to see him as he was her.

****

Martha Henry stood with her dashing new beau at the bar and she made it obvious for any who cared to see that he belonged to her and she to him. They engaged in getting even better acquainted when Martha observed John Brewer making his way toward them. Brewer had once been her lover and now menacingly approached from behind the man who was still insisting he was Bob Smith.

John Brewer's reputation ran far and wide as a ruffian who few men would dare cross. Even a man of Bob Smith's height would be forced to look up at the towering Brewer who additionally stretched broad across the chest and shoulders with thick muscles. Brewer also mastered considerable skill with his handgun and seldom hesitated to display the skill. Brewer walked right up behind Bob Smith and tapped him sternly on the shoulder with a huge index finger.

Bob Smith turned and looked up into the scowling face of John Brewer.

"The way you wear those Navy Colts in that sash, boy," Brewer snarled, "is the same way Hickok preferred to wear his iron. Are you trying to imitate old Wild Bill?"

"I imitate no man," Bob Smith replied calmly.

"Looks to me, too, boy, as if you took that jacket and vest from your daddy's closet. They're a tad big for you. You like playing dress up, boy?" Brewer grinned as he reached out and rubbed the lapel of Smith's frock coat between a thumb and index finger.

"If you care to keep that hand," Smith grinned back while standing calmly with his hands folded behind his back, "you'll remove it from my clothing."

Martha suddenly experienced both fear and excitement. Her new young man would surely be no match for John Brewer, but she could not find it in herself to interfere. Men engaging in combat always thrilled her, and nothing told more about a man than how he handled himself in a fight.

Brewer did not remove his thumb and finger from the lapel, but closed his entire hand around the lapel and jerked Smith up on his toes bringing him face to face. Smith's right hand came up from behind his back, and before Brewer could say or do more, Smith put a Remington Double Derringer firmly against the cheek and just below the left eye of the much larger man.

"Ever seen what damage one of these can do up close when both barrels go off?" Smith chuckled. "It makes a real mess. Now, unhand me."

Smith applied so much pressure that Brewer's head cocked upward. A more prudent man would back off a step or two. Of course, Martha knew Brewer to be too proud and stubborn of an ass to admit he'd been bested by not much more than a kid. Brewer didn't back off but he did drop his hand from Smith's jacket.

"If we had not been in the presence of a lady," Smith said with a straight and serious expression, "you would now be dead."

"There will be another time," Brewer growled.

"I take that as a threat," Smith hummed before smoothly pulling one of the big revolver's from his sash with his free hand and landing it hard upside Brewer's skull. The big man stumbled back and dropped his bleeding head into his hands. Smith raised the gun high over his own head and brought it crashing down on the top of Brewer's.

John Brewer toppled to his knees and might have remained longer in that position had Smith not placed a boot in his chest to shove him over backwards. Brewer twitched a couple of times before falling unconscious.

Smith tucked the derringer back in place and extracted the other big Navy Colt from his sash. With one elevated in each hand, he slowly turned around the packed room and said with a most cocky grin, "Does this man have a friend that wishes to step up in his stead?"

Martha recalled Brewer having a number of friends, but apparently none so dear as to serve as his proxy.

CHAPTER NINE

Didn't Twitch Another Muscle

Babb barely got the Colts back in the sash before Martha had him by the arm in order to drag him up the stairs. Once in the room, Babb submitted and she practically did all else. The woman unleashed her desires to consume Babb like a hungry hound on a biscuit.

"It was the bravado," she admitted a few minutes later after rolling off the top of a very spent Babb. "A brave and dangerous man does things to me. Well, you saw what it did to me!"

Babb certainly did. Maybe he'd just lay here about five or so minutes and go back downstairs and best another man. He derived great pleasure from clubbing that big bastard. Martha's contribution served as icing on the cake.

"And if it should ever happen again," Martha panted, "that you should find yourself in need of killing a man, don't put it off on my behalf."

"Why, Martha," Babb grinned and winked, "are you saying you'd enjoy watching me kill a man?"

"Have you killed before?" she asked wide-eyed as she rolled up on an elbow to stare into his face.

"I've killed before," he nodded, holding her stare with his own.

Martha closed her eyes, took a deep breath and shuddered just so slightly. When she opened her eyes she crawled in close and cooed, "Tell me all about it, Bob Smith."

"First, madam," Babb teased, "I think we've reached a point in this relationship where you deserve to know my true name."

"Oh! It's not Bob Smith?" Martha giggled.

"No ma'am," he chuckled at her obvious ribbing, "my name is Dallas Babb."

Martha scowled as if thinking hard and then shot upright in the bed, "Dallas Babb? But you're no coward!"

Babb shot up beside her. "Why hell no, I'm no coward. Where did you come up with that?"

"I read it in the newspapers. I've been reading about you and... "

"My name was in the papers?" Babb asked somewhat hopeful, although this coward thing could prove troublesome.

"In bunches of them. I read how you robbed a bank with some brothers named... let me think... "

"Mosier," Babb inserted.

"Yes, Mosier, and how you took the money by shooting one of the brothers in the back... "

"In the back of the head," Babb objected, "but just because he was running away from me. It wasn't as if I snuck up and back shot him. Is some reporter calling me a coward for that?"

"No. It isn't a reporter that said you are cowardly. It was... " Martha scrunched her face in concentration,

"... Bardoe. That's his name, Clay Bardoe. It's him that's called you a coward."

"Clay Bardoe?" Babb exclaimed. "Why, Clay's my kin. What's Uncle Clay have to do with any of this?"

Martha took a deep breath and appeared to be getting the facts straight in her memory. "After the Mosier brothers and those other two men killed Bardoe's wife... "

"Millie?" Babb interrupted. "Millie is dead?"

"She died terribly," Martha clucked. "Bardoe has already killed all but one of the Mosiers and those other two men and…"

"I need to read those papers," Babb said as he climbed from the bed.

"I can try and rake them up," Martha offered.

"You do that," Babb said in a huff.

****

Mathew Baker felt out of place because of his youth and bare feet and bibbed overalls. Still, though, he made it through the swinging doors and couldn't stop now. His ma could use the money and all that land.

The rough looking customers in the Drover's paid him much attention as Mathew padded on toward the table way in the back. He could see the lone man sitting back there, and that man stared hard in his direction.

"Mr. Bardoe?" Mathew managed only after clearing his throat.

"What business you have in this place, boy?"

"I'm looking for Mr. Clay Bardoe," Mathew nearly gagged.

"You've found him."

Mathew couldn't help but look at the eyes. He'd been in church every Sunday since he could remember and knew a fair deal about the devil. If this man wasn't the devil, you couldn't tell it by looking in those eyes. Two large guns lay on the table along with one very serious knife. Bardoe's hands rested to the right and left of the assembly of killing tools. The hands remained as still as rock.

"My name is Mathew Baker," the boy stammered.

"That's a good enough name," the man with the glaring eyes nodded. "So, tell me, Mathew Baker, what are you doing standing in front of my table?"

Mathew tried to keep his knees from knocking, but he couldn't. "I found Bob Mosier today," he confessed. "And I'm here to tell you where you can find him."

"And you know," Bardoe said in a very calm way, "when you tell me, that I'm going to go kill him?"

"Yes, Sir."

"Then tell me, boy."

****

Babb spent the entire day reading over and over the papers Martha gathered and brought to him in her room. It took him a while, but he eventually wrapped his brain around all that had so far taken place. The Mosiers and Wade and that half-breed Charlie had gone to Bardoe's home to confront Millicent Bardoe on Babb's whereabouts. The reasons they had not gone to the general store and directly to Clay Bardoe were obvious even to Babb.

In the process of gathering information on Babb, the gang of idiots succumbed to their desires for the beautiful Millie, and did then and there, have their way with her and left her dead. Since that time, Clay Bardoe had done an overly sufficient job of killing Charlie, Wade, and Leroy Mosier.

The ways and means the Mosiers and Wade and Charlie had killed Millicent Bardoe, along with the ways and means Clay Bardoe so far revenged her death, had attracted the attention of the newspapers and periodicals.

In those accountings, Bardoe professed he would kill all responsible, including Dallas Babb. And in those professions Bardoe declared over and over again that the hardest to kill would be Babb for the simple reason Babb would run to the world's end to escape the punishment he deserved. In short, and very distinctly, Bardoe called Dallas Babb a slimy, conniving, and sniveling coward in front of the entire reading West. In some publications he used those very words.

Babb threw the last of the papers aside, rose to his feet, and started gathering his belongings.

"What are you doing, Dallas?" the very attentive Martha asked.

"No man calls me a coward without accounting for his words. Not even my Uncle Clay."

"Are you going to that town… Stillwater?" Martha asked.

"That's where I'm headed. I can't kill him from here."

Martha moved in close. "This will be a duel they will write and talk about for years to come. Take me with you, Dallas. I have a fine buggy. We could ride in style."

"You can go with me," Babb smiled, "but it won't be that much of a fight. I'm better with a pistol than Uncle Clay ever hoped to be. Hell, he's told me that himself."

Martha practically leapt into Babb's arms. "Oh, Dallas, this is an adventure of a lifetime. When do we leave?"

"First thing in the morning. So, we better turn in. It's a fair piece to Stillwater."

They turned in, but Martha apparently had more than sleep on her mind.

****

Bob Mosier stepped out of the cabin long before sunup. It should have been darker, but a full moon still clinging to the western skyline lit the earth like a dimly glowing coal-oil lamp. Enough light shone, in fact, that Mosier had no trouble noticing the horse and rider sitting idle on a not so distant knoll overlooking the Mosier homestead.

Mosier took in a long breath through his nostrils and let it out slowly through his lips. As if everything existed just hunky-dory, he casually strolled to the barn and saddled his horse. He led his horse out of the barn to find the man on the knoll still in place and still watching. Mosier mounted up and chose west for the direction to ride. He kept his horse at a walk. His old mount was sturdy, but not at all fast. Running would be simply a waste of time and energy for both him and his horse. He traveled a distance of a hundred or so yards before looking over his shoulder. The big and light colored horse and his master just kept pace – following, but making no effort to quickly overtake their prey.

Mosier would ride a little while and then look back. Each time the man behind him drew just a little bit closer. Mosier felt toyed with, but what could he do about that? Turn and fight? It wouldn't be much of a fight. He just kept on keeping on and figured that the presence to his rear would catch up whenever the man on the pale horse wanted to.

Mosier made it a decent distance from his parents' place when Clay Bardoe pulled alongside. Both men rode side by side for a fair piece without speaking or even looking in each other's direction. Bardoe held the upper hand by virtue of his killing skills, and he spoke first.

"I've come to believe that you did my wife no harm."

****

Clay Bardoe waited for a response. Both men and their horses traveled several yards before it came.

"I also did her no good," Mosier sighed.

"Yup."

A few more yards and a few more minutes elapsed before Bardoe said, "If you'd killed that boy, I wouldn't be here beside you right now."

For the first time since they'd been riding side by side, Bardoe turned to look at Mosier. He didn't look back. His eyes stared at the path before him.

"You'd caught up with me sooner or later. Besides, it ain't in me to kill a mere boy."

They rode quite a distance before Bardoe said, "There are worse things in life than dying… for men like you and me."

"Yeah, I can't help but agree," Mosier nodded emphatically. "Worse things such as… living."

Mercifully quick, Bardoe pulled the gun on his right hip with his left hand and put a single bullet into Bob Mosier's brain.

Mosier fell from his horse, and the horse kept going. Bardoe reined his to a halt and dismounted. The last of the Mosier boys came to rest on his left side. Bardoe used the toe of his boot to gently roll Mosier over on his back. He pushed his hat back on his head as he squatted down next to the body. For the longest time he did nothing but stare into the face of the dead man while wondering if God might someday have pity on him like he had on Bob Mosier.

****

The sun perched high and bright in the sky by the time Bardoe rounded up Mosier's horse and got Mosier thrown across the saddle. No one stirred outside the squatty Mosier cabin. Bardoe expected the old man had already taken to toiling in the fields. The old woman more than likely busied herself inside doing whatever old women do. Bardoe rode up to the front of the cabin and hollered out.

"Hello inside the house!"

The door slowly swung open and the old woman stepped onto the front porch with her shotgun at the ready. She trained the barrel on Bardoe while her eyes fell heavily upon the body lying limp over the saddle.

"You've taken my last one from me," she mumbled.

Bardoe removed his hat. "Your boys set their own course, Missus Mosier. I don't regret what I've done to them, but I do regret the pain you've been caused."

The old woman turned her pale cold hard eyes from the body to Bardoe. She pulled the hammer back on the shotgun. "You've left me no more tears to cry. My last boy lies there dead and I can't shed a single tear. I think I'll kill you for that, Clay Bardoe."

"I won't be allowing you to do that today, ma'am. I got one more man to kill before the debt for my wife's death is paid. When I've done that, bring your shotgun to town and you can have at me."

Ma Mosier took considerable time to chew on Bardoe's words before lowering her shotgun. "I won't be coming after you and neither will my old man. Leaving you to live will be a greater punishment than taking your life."

Bardoe put his hat back on his head and nodded to the spoken truth before saying,

"Missus Mosier, I need to know if you want me to take Bob into town and let Sid Rowden prepare him for burial… or do you just want me to leave him with you now?"

Ma Mosier stepped down from the porch and took a minute or two to look closely at her son's body.

"You didn't mess my Bob up."

"No, ma'am. He didn't deserve being messed up. He only deserved being dead. He didn't suffer."

The old woman struggled back upon her porch and studied Bardoe a second or two before saying, "He already dug his own grave. I'd appreciate it if you'd just take him out back and put him in it."

****

CB Wooly stepped off the train in Guthrie to find Walt Tabor waiting on his arrival. Wooly smiled at the sight of his friend, but the smile quickly dwindled away.

"Walt? Where are your guns? Where's your badge?" Tabor stood dressed in a sack suit like some kind of bank teller or clerk.

"CB, I threw them down in Miss Laura's whore house in Stillwater and walked away from them. As far as I know, they may still be there today."

"Why, hell, Walt, why would you do that?"

"Truth is, CB, I'm a coward of little worth, and I owe it to you to let you hear it from my own mouth. That's why I'm here today."

Wooly pulled his hat off and scratched at his graying hair. "I've rode with you near three years now, Walt, and I ain't never seen you perform a cowardly act."

The much younger man in his ill-fitting townie clothes looked down and shuffled the gravel at his feet with his lace up boots. "That's because you ain't never seen me go up against Clay Bardoe."

Wooly's stomach seemed to do a flip-flop inside his body.

"What happened between you and Clay?"

"I'd been trying to keep an eye on him, and I watched him walk out of the Drover's with a clear purpose in mind late one night. So, I followed him to Miss Laura's because it was for sure he was about to kill someone. He was going up the stairs when I called his name and tried to get him to let the law do its job.

"It was Leroy Mosier he sought, and he told me there wasn't a darn thing that was going to stop him. He then allowed me to pull my pistol, cock it, and point it at him. He said he'd give me the first shot, but if I didn't put him down, he'd shoot me dead. That's when I tossed my iron and my badge on the floor."

"How far were you standing from Clay?" Wooly asked.

"A good forty paces."

"Why, hell, Walt, in the swell of a fight, it'd be damned hard at that distance to take a man out with just one round. I know of only one human that can for sure do it, and that's the man you was facing. I think you did a damned smart thing."

"You wouldn't have done it," Walt sighed.

"Yeah, well, I ain't all that smart."

Walt Tabor stood with his head hanging, and Wooly tried to come up with words that would make him feel better about what he'd done. But in all honesty, there existed no such words. When a man like Tabor backed down from another man, things inside him became too bruised for words to help. Wooly went on to other things.

"Did he kill Leroy Mosier?"

"Beat him to death. Then he shot and killed a whore that was there in the room with Mosier. That's another reason I'm here. A warrant's been issued for Bardoe over the murdering of that woman."

Wooly remained silent as he digested all that information. It damned sure wasn't like Clay Bardoe to harm a woman, much less kill one. Wooly came to the conclusion that once a man like Bardoe started to kill, it didn't matter to him who or what he killed.

"You know, CB," Tabor said to get back his attention, "it'll more than likely be you that has to serve that warrant."

CB Wooly slowly and solemnly nodded his head, "More than likely so."

****

Bardoe reigned Moonshine to a stop several feet shy of the front porch to the small Victorian house he'd shared with Millicent. The house now belonged to Miss Laura, but it still sat vacant. Some parts of Bardoe wanted to dismount and take one final walk through the house. Many more parts of him kept him in the saddle.

Bardoe stared at the front door and he thought of the many days she'd met him at that door with an enthusiastic hug and a kiss. Of all those many times, that had been one of the highlights of his day. He found her for the last time just inside that door. Bardoe shook the horrid memory from his mind and concentrated instead on the laughter and love they shared beyond the front door. Things they did and things she said came to him in memory.

Bardoe listened for only a few minutes to the words and wonders of the past before they became too burdensome. He wheeled Moonshine away from the house and left at a trot, resisting the urges to look back. He rode his horse into town and hitched him to a fence post in front of the cemetery. He'd not been to the grave, but knew the location of Millicent's family plot. Not near enough time had passed for grass to cover the mounded earth.

Bardoe removed his hat and cleared his throat. "I've repaid the debt to the men that took your life, Millie. I intend soon to get the one whose actions caused those men to do… " He stumbled for a word to describe what they did, "… that terrible deed."

After that, Bardoe would have nothing left to live for except the day he could join his Millie in peaceful rest.

****

Martha stepped out of the Peacock and into the light of day with Dallas Babb on her arm. She wore her traveling clothes and her servants already loaded a trunk onto the back of her coach. Earlier she made arrangements to have Babb's magnificent white horse groomed and hitched to the back of her conveyance.

"Well, I do swear, Martha," Babb grinned, "that is one fine buggy. Don't know that I've ever traveled in such luxury."

"It comes all the way from Mifflinburg, Pennsylvania," Martha responded proudly. "I had it custom built by the Coachmaker William A. Heiss."

"I've heard of the Heiss buggy, but never thought I'd be riding in one," he nodded.

"Well, I never thought I'd be going on such a high adventure with a dapper young gentleman," Martha cooed. "Just once more, Dallas, do tell me how it's all going to happen. It thrills me so!"

Babb threw back his head and laughed, but then got in character with a most serious look on his handsome face. "I'm going to let you go in the Drover's Saloon first and by yourself. You'll be able to identify Clay by how all them papers says he sits in that far corner with his weapons laid out on the table. You'll stroll right in and pick out a prime seat so you got a bird's eye view of both Clay and the front door.

"I'll give you a few minutes, and then I'll do some strolling my own self. I'm going to walk in that place like I own it," Babb said as he demonstrated a proud stride in a circle on the plank sidewalk in front of the Peacock.

Martha giggled in delight. Her young man could certainly strut, and the sound of his spurs jingling and his boot heels pounding on the board walk sent goose bumps up and down both arms.

"I'll have my arms down at my sides like I do now when I first walk in. I'll take a few steps, locate Clay, and then I'll fold my arms up like this." Babb struck a pose with his legs shoulder width apart, his head held high, and his arms crossed on his chest.

That stance along with the look on his face caused Martha to reach out to a nearby lamp post to support her trembling knees.

"I'm going to look him hard and square in the eyes, and I'm going to shout out, 'Uncle Clay Bardoe, you have soiled my reputation and I've come here to put a bullet through your lying head!'"

In the next blink of an eye, Babb's arms dropped and his hands grasped the handles of the Navy Colts in the sash.

"Then I'll just grab these here Colts and shoot him dead as yesterday."

Martha gripped the post even harder as Babb stepped up close and winked down at her. She opened her mouth to shriek delight when a chunk of the lamp post next to Babb's head splintered and the sound of gunfire rang out. Martha wanted to run or duck or do anything to take herself out of the line of fire, but her body simply would not move. Babb displayed no such problem. He was moving, but he wasn't running or ducking. Instead, he strode deliberately toward the direction of the gunfire and the lone figure of big John Brewer.

Brewer stood across the street and up on the opposing sidewalk at least fifty paces away. He held a single revolver at shoulder level and took aim for a second shot. Babb already stepped off the plank walk and started into the street. His palms and fingers gripped the handles of the Colts, but they remained in the sash. Brewer pulled the trigger a second time and dirt kicked up at Babb's feet, but it didn't seem to faze him. He kept going until he reached the middle of the street.

Brewer got off a third round, and Martha didn't see where it hit, but it didn't hit Babb. Before Brewer got another try,

Babb, standing tall and erect with his feet planted shoulder width apart, calmly pulled both revolvers from the sash, leveled them at his waist and started cocking the hammers and pulling the triggers.

From Martha's position she couldn't tell that Babb's bullets struck anything but John Brewer. The sturdy man looked as if he were taking powerful punches from an invisible fist. Initially, the impact of the lead pushed him backwards several steps and then he toppled backwards and didn't twitch another muscle.

The next thing Martha knew, Babb assisted her into the carriage.

"That was clearly an act of self-defense on my part," Babb said with nothing in his tone betraying the fact he'd just nearly been killed and had killed, "but we best not tarry here. The last thing I need to do is talk to the law."

Martha trembled, but not entirely from fear. She'd never witnessed an act so thrilling or a man so brave. She sat as close as possible to her man. He quickly maneuvered the buggy out of Wichita and south toward the Oklahoma Territory.

CHAPTER TEN

An Instinctive Killer

C B Wooly picked up the warrant for Clay Bardoe's arrest at the courthouse and bought a bottle of whiskey from the saloon across the street. He took both back to Missus Gertrude Stem's boarding house and up to the second floor room he had rented for nearly two years.

Wooly settled into the small room's only chair with a shot glass, the bottle, and a legal document that authorized him to take into custody a man he'd often considered the best friend he ever had. Wooly gazed at the warrant for only a few seconds before tossing it aside. Other than the implications and potential complications, it read no different than the hundreds of warrants he'd served over the many years he'd been a lawman. Wooly did not intend so quickly to put aside the shot glass and bottle.

After uncorking and then filling the small glass, Wooly held the glass high, sighed, and said to nobody but himself, "Here's to you, Clay."

He threw the first glass back and poured a second. It too went into the air. "Here's to me, Clay." And down the second one went.

Wooly poured a third and at that point started to sip. Sipping always went better with reminiscing. If Wooly continued to throw entire gulps of the fiery liquid to the back of his throat, all he remembered about Bardoe and, therefore, all he knew about Bardoe, would soon get boggled in his mind. It proved too hard to study what a man, based on his past, might or might not do... in a given situation... if the studier had a boggled mind.

CB Wooly could tell stories about Clay Bardoe all day long and half way into the night. The two men had encountered about every kind of bad man who the Wild West had to offer. They'd brought in Indians from about a dozen different tribes, Mexicans, all kinds of whites, and even men with black skin who had once been slaves. They stood and watched a fair number of their prisoners hang from the neck on the order of Judge Isaac Parker, and some men they'd pursued died before getting a chance to appear before Judge Parker. That had always been because Wooly killed them.

One particular situation seemed to jump to the forefront of Wooly's mind. Back in the mid '70's two old boys who had been the closest of friends since fighting for Grant at Vicksburg took to terrorizing the Chickasaws in and around Tishomingo.

Those who knew Tom Hill and Samuel Brewster would tell that they were closer than any two brothers ever had been. No man ever fought one without having to fight the other at the very same time. A good man might beat either one of them one on one, but the best of men couldn't beat the two of them together. They were both skilled fighters with about any weapon they could lay their hands on, and both meaner than a bull thumped in the gonads. They shared the best time robbing and shooting the citizenry of the Chickasaw Nation until both happened to fall head over heels for the same little gal.

Wooly and Bardoe combed the territory for months looking for the thieving and murdering duo. They'd heard all the stories about how Hill and Brewster were thicker than molasses, so it came as a great surprise when they learned Brewster had killed Hill with a chopping axe. It seemed that the one sure-fire thing that has forever been capable of destroying the harmony between men... a woman... had brought to an end a notorious friendship.

The deputy U.S. marshals finally caught up with Samuel Brewster at a popular crossing on the Canadian River. Bardoe had been shaky sick with the chills since two days prior, so it fell solely upon Wooly to take on Brewster.

Brewster already made it to the north bank when the two lawmen spotted him and began to ford the river from the south bank. The outlaw had a considerable head start, and the ailing Bardoe could do little more than stay upright in the saddle. Wooly quickly pulled away from his partner in his efforts to keep the wanted man from escaping.

Wooly rode a fresh mount and Brewster evidently did not. The deputy gained quickly as the outlaw's horse stepped into a gopher hole and went from a full out gallop to flipping and rolling. Brewster flew over the horse's head and rolled one direction while his pistol shot out of his holster and tumbled another direction. Wooly remained far enough away at that moment that Brewster could have easily recovered his gun had the horse not rolled over him.

The bulk of the horse did not tumble squarely over the top of Brewster or he'd been squashed like a turd on a trail. He sustained just enough hurt to daze him, and he groped around on the ground for his pistol until Wooly drew near. Wooly jumped down from his horse and pulled his rifle from the scabbard. By that time Brewster had eyed his firearm and reached for it.

Wooly worked his lever to chamber a round and took a bead on Brewster. "Samuel Brewster, leave that gun be!" Wooly shouted. He guessed at the time that only twelve to fifteen feet of ground separated the two of them.

Brewster momentarily headed the warning, but by the way he shook his head to clear his thinking, Wooly felt certain the other man had not given up the idea of arming himself. Wooly could see out the corner of his eye that Bardoe had arrived, but slumped in the saddle and gripped the saddle horn just to keep from falling to the ground. Sure enough, after a little more head shaking, Brewster started again inching on all fours toward his revolver.

"This is your last warning, Samuel. Roll over and put your arms up in the air."

Wooly never figured out if old Samuel Brewster was just too rum dumb, just dumb, or exceedingly stubborn, but he kept on going for that pistol.

The very second he wrapped his fingers around the handle, Wooly pulled his trigger. The bullet connected with a spot just above Brewster's left ear and ripped the top part of his head from the bottom part.

Early that following evening Wooly built a fire and helped Bardoe to a place real close to it. After he had some supper and laid there for a couple of hours, Bardoe started to shake loose from the grips of his illness. Before bedtime he turned quite vocal.

"CB, you didn't have to kill that darned Brewster," Bardoe said as he nodded in the direction of the hobbled horse which was bearing the weight of the dead body. "Hell, he was close enough and feeble enough that you could have just run up and kicked the gun out of his reach, or even ran up and clubbed him down with the butt of your rifle."

Wooly had considered such, and he'd already prepared a defense for his partner's inevitable charges. "Yeah, and what if he'd just been joshing, Clay? What if he'd just been putting on an act? Playing possum just so I'd take my eyes from my sights for just a split second? Shoot fire, my friend, the moment I started to run up to him, he could've leapt for that gun and rolled and put a bullet in me."

"I think he was honestly dazed," Bardoe said.

"Yeah, but you don't know that for sure, and neither did I."

"At the very least, at that distance, you could have shot him in the leg or even in the fat of the ass. I have never seen a man whose ass wasn't bigger than his head anyway. You hit Brewster in the head, so you could have hit him in the ass," Bardoe countered.

Wooly presented yet another prepared response. "Clay, you know damned good and well that not all men can shoot like you. You particularly know I can't. Most men, like myself, can expect to get one shot and only one shot and that damned one shot better count. Say I did aim at his leg and just nicked him, or that I hit him and it didn't take him down. By the time I could have chambered another round, he could have had his gun in his hand. Why, hell, then it would have been a toss-up. No, sir, if I have to shoot, I'm expecting one shot, and I'm aiming to make that one count. I ain't never seen a dead man yet that can shoot back, but a wounded man with a gun is about a dangerous a thing a law man can encounter."

Wooly paused to let Bardoe counter. When it appeared his partner could level no further accusations, Wooly let go again.

"You know, Clay Bardoe, you stay in this line of work long enough, you'll end up having to kill a man."

"I been in it a good spell already," Bardoe grinned. "Ain't killed one yet."

"Uh-huh, but a day will come. You can mark my words."

"That day may very well come, CB. But I've told you before that when it is an important enough goings-on, I'll kill a man, but it's going to have to be damned important that I do. I don't want death haunting my sleep."

Wooly yawned long and hard and chuckled before saying, "Maybe I should, but I ain't never had a problem with a damned thing interfering with my sleep."

"You are a hard man, CB Wooly," Bardoe clucked.

Wooly stretched out on his bedroll and started to doze when Bardoe called his name.

"Yup?" Wooly grunted.

"Them two old boys had been darn good friends for a long time."

"That's what I hear tell."

"Why, heck, that would be like you or me turning one on the other."

"We ain't outlaws."

"Yeah, but we're good friends."

"I'd never turn on you, Clay. Hell that would be about a stupid thing to do. I couldn't take you head on and couldn't stand shooting you in the back."

"I've thought this over, CB. I think if it came down between me and you in a life or death situation, you'd be the one walking away."

"You reckon? That doesn't make any sense to me. You're a better shot and calmer under fire than I am."

"Yeah, but CB, you are an instinctive killer. My instinct is to wound. If we was to go up against each other because of some profound hatred, I'd wound you. Then you'd heal, and I might have to wound you again, but eventually, you'd end up killing me. It's just in our nature. I wouldn't kill you and you wouldn't quit until you did kill me."

That had been back in the '70's, and a lot had changed since them days. Just maybe, Wooly thought as he continued to sip his whiskey, ol' Clay Bardoe had been predicting the future, but not with complete accuracy. Clay had digressed to more of a killer than Wooly had ever thought of being. That simply meant Wooly did not expect to fair well going up against his old friend. Not well at all.

Tomorrow, or the next day, or even the next, depending on how this bottle of whiskey and maybe others to follow so moved him, Wooly would ride to Stillwater and try to talk Bardoe into giving up peacefully and allow Wooly to take him into custody. If Bardoe insisted in making a fight of it, CB Wooly expected to be killed outright.

****

Babb stared into the embers of their campfire until Martha interrupted his concentration.

"You appear to be lost in thought," she said as she took a seat next to him on the fallen tree that marked the spot where they decided to stop for the night.

"I am," he nodded.

"About what?"

"Killing my Uncle Clay."

"Are you starting to believe you should do otherwise?"

"Nope. Still got to kill him, but it is a pity. I do owe the man a good deal of gratitude."

Babb listened a minute or two to the night noises before extending his legs out in front of him and settling into a comfortable story telling position.

"My old daddy was a mean son of a bitch. I think the man hated pretty much everything, but nothing more than he did me and my mama. My earliest memories are of his fists falling on top of my head. I thought it was pretty much a common thing to be beaten, or to watch him beat my mama. I thought it was just what every man did, but my mama told me that wasn't so.

"She'd told me about her brother, Clay Bardoe. He was a different kind of man, she said. The stories she told made the man bigger than life in my little boy head. I enjoyed thinking that I had an uncle that was a famed deputy U.S. marshal. Hell, if someone was to tell me the stories now that she told me then, I'd know for sure they was trying to sell me a pig in a polk.

"I didn't lay eyes on the man until around my sixth year. That was a while ago, but I can still remember it as if it was yesterday. I was out in the barnyard when I spotted the horse and rider approaching. We didn't get a lot of company out where we lived and it was a treat when we did. I can remember being able to tell at a distance that the horse wasn't your everyday run of the mill horse and its owner was no saddle tramp. Both the man and animal were just as proud looking as kings," he marveled.

"Once I made out what the rider was wearing, I knew who he was. He was dressed just like my mama told in her stories. From the top of his pointy hat to the blunt tips of his fancy boots, my Uncle Clay looked like everything I'd always imagined he would be. Even before the man spoke a word, I knew I'd be awfully fond of him. Even now, my heart thumps hard when I think how he reined that horse to a halt and looked down from the saddle and said... "

****

"Boy, I'd guess your name is Dallas Babb,"

It took Dallas a minute to find his voice. Even then he forced the two word reply from his mouth. "Yes, sir." And he'd yet to look this man in the face. His attention had first been focused on the sleek black horse. Now, at eye level, he admired the richly tanned leather of the rider's left stove-top boot, and the ornate silver spur attached to the boot.

"Would you happen to know who I am?" the man asked.

Dallas averted his eyes momentarily from the man's tack and apparel to look up and into a lively pair of pale blue eyes that squinted against the bright light of day.

"Yes, sir," he managed once again.

"Then call my name, Dallas," the man said with a friendly grin.

"You'd be my Uncle Clay Bardoe."

"That's sure enough who I am," Bardoe chuckled.

Young Dallas nearly went cross-eyed trying to take in his uncle's finery. He'd never seen a long gun with shiny brass on it like the rifle in the scabbard. His daddy had an old cap and ball pistol with marred and scarred walnut grips. Two pistols with smooth and white handles peaked from beneath Uncle Clay's black frock coat. On that frock coat dangled a silvery medallion signifying to even a young boy that it set this man apart from others. Topping it all off sat the hat on his head. The color of cream, it bore evenly shaped indentions circling a crown that came to a rounded point above the indentions and a brim that didn't have a bit of sag or droop to it.

"Ma always said you'd come this way one day and I'd get to meet you," Dallas said, and even added a grin of his own.

"And here I am just like she said. Ma's are smart things, aren't they?"

"Yes, sir," Dallas said with the grin still plastered in place. His ma also said Uncle Clay had hunted down and put in jail some of the orneriest outlaws in the Oklahoma Territory. Dallas could not remember being happier. But then his pa's voice rang out.

"I don't take to having the law on my place," he shouted as he stepped from the barn and started toward Bardoe and Dallas.

Bardoe sat calmly and didn't respond until the elder Babb stomped close enough so that he could do so without raising his voice. "I mean no offense. I was in the area and just stopped by to see my sister and her boy."

"He's my boy, too," Babb growled.

"Kind of works that way, don't it?" Bardoe grinned with good-natured ease. "Every boy has a pa somewhere."

"Are you poking fun at me?" Babb scowled.

"It's not in my nature to do such, Mr. Babb."

"He's just being friendly, Pa," Dallas threw in, and immediately wished he hadn't.

"You got those eggs gathered yet, boy?" Babb spat.

"No, sir, I was... "

No words could follow before his father grabbed him by the scruff of the neck and started kicking him in the butt with his heavy work boots. Dallas wanted to let out a howl but would not do so in front of his uncle. After three or four mighty kicks, the father shook the son viciously before throwing him to the ground and pinning him there with a boot pressed down hard on his chest. Within seconds Dallas gasped to catch his air.

"It's also not in my nature to interfere with how a man deals with his son..." Bardoe called down from his horse,

"… unless that man is dealing with his son in a manner I find too awful. Let the boy up, Mr. Babb."

Babb just pressed down harder. "Don't no man tell me how to deal with my family."

Bardoe swung out of his saddle before announcing in a hiss, "This man does. Let the boy up, Babb."

Babb lifted his boot from Dallas's chest. But then just to show he could, he let go with a terrible kick that caught the boy in the side of his ribs. This time Dallas could not help but yelp in pain. What happened next took more time to tell than it did to occur.

Dallas' pa stood a head taller and weighed much more than the slender uncle. To bring all matters even, Bardoe pulled one of his pistols, flipped it in his hand to grab the cylinder and then drove the butt of the gun right into the middle of Babb's glaring eyeballs. The bigger man staggered back a step or two before Bardoe hammered him again, splitting his nose like a rotten tomato. With practiced ease, Bardoe slipped the gun quickly back into his holster while almost at the very moment throwing his other fisted hand into the mess he'd already made of Babb's nose.

Babb brought both hands up to grab his ruined face while Bardoe put first a right and then a left into the exposed rib cage. Babb grunted like a stuck pig and groaned in pain like a wedding night virgin when Bardoe hit him twice more. The final blows caused Babb's knees to buckle and he collapsed to the ground.

"Where is your ma, Dallas?" Bardoe said in a voice not the least taxed by the physical effort.

"She's in the house."

"You go in there with her," Bardoe nodded, "and you both stay in there until I make my way up there."

Dallas took off in a run with his lungs still burning from a lack of air. He stumbled into the house to find his ma watching all from her kitchen window. He joined her there to watch the rest.

Bardoe squatted down next to the prone man and began mouthing words Dallas could only imagine. For what seemed like the longest time, Bardoe's lips moved as Babb's head seemed to nod in agreement to whatever was being said. Dallas knew all that needed to be said had been said when Bardoe helped Babb to his feet, pointed to the north, and stood and watched as Babb took off in that direction. When Babb faded out of sight, Bardoe started for the house with his horse following on his heels.

Dallas didn't know his pa's destination and didn't want to. If his ma cared one iota about her husband leaving, she didn't show it. Wherever he went, he never came back from there, and no man ever again put a boot or a hand to him or his ma.

****

The more Dallas said the heavier Martha's heart grew. She listened intently as Dallas explained that from that day on, Clay Bardoe came to mean more to Dallas than his own father ever had. Long periods of time might pass before Bardoe returned to their home in Missouri, but when he visited, he spent all the time he could with his young nephew. From what Martha gathered, Bardoe taught Dallas the things all boys needed to learn to fit into manhood.

Their best times together, she gleaned, centered on Bardoe putting his own guns into Dallas's hands and showing him the ways and means to make the most of them. He taught him the proper way to aim and squeeze a trigger and, more importantly, how to shoot what needed shot without having to aim. According to Dallas, Bardoe had on more than one occasion marveled on an instinctive shooting ability that surpassed even that of Bardoe's practiced skills. The uncle even bought the nephew his first gun and presented it to him on his sixteenth birthday.

Martha learned how, during Bardoe's long absences, Dallas practiced daily with that gun and how it soon became common knowledge that young Dallas Babb would one day be a force few men would want to challenge. Dallas said when he turned eighteen, Bardoe encouraged him to pin on a badge.

By that time, Bardoe's absences had been too long and his visits too few. Dallas Babb had developed into his own kind of man, and not the kind of man suited to wear a badge. He declined his uncle's offer, and the two men grew apart thereafter.

Once Dallas said all he intended to say, Martha sighed and shook her head. The entire accounting left her feeling lower than an ant's belly.

"We should be turning back toward Wichita in the morn," she mumbled without trying to hide her sorrow.

"Why would we do such a thing?" Dallas asked.

"You obviously cannot now kill your uncle."

"The hell I can't," Dallas huffed.

Martha grabbed her man and gave him a loving hug as her

lowly feeling seemed to be lifted on the wings of a great soaring bird. "Oh, Dallas," she cooed, "I feared our great adventure had come to an unsatisfying conclusion!"

CHAPTER ELEVEN

The Thumping Finger

Bardoe and everyone else in the Drover's paid notice when the fancy dressed and seemingly highborn woman strode into the saloon. By her clothes she didn't belong, but the look on her face and the easy way she moved, said to all that she was no stranger to places predominantly visited by men and shunned by the more refined.

It seemed equally evident to Bardoe that she'd come there on his account. She'd readily located him with her eyes as if she knew exactly where to find him. But why she took a table far to one side instead of approaching him with her business, he did not know. Being a woman, and one of some means, maybe she needed time to consider or even reconsider the reasons that brought her there. Bardoe never assumed to fully understand a woman, particularly a woman who would walk unescorted into an establishment like the Drover's.

Even though Bardoe intentionally stared hard in her direction, once she took a seat, she paid him no never mind. Over the past couple of days there had been more than a few strangers who had entered the saloon just to get a glimpse of the subject of so many recent newspaper articles.

Long ago as a lawman, he grew astounded how normally good citizens would flock around a notorious killer. In that he'd become such, he deemed the woman just another curiosity seeker come for no other reason than being able to one day say, "I went to see Clay Bardoe sitting at that table in the far corner of the Drover's Saloon."

After several minutes passed without the woman making a move, Bardoe turned his thoughts from her to what remained of his business. He hoped this woman, like the curious others before her, would have news on the whereabouts of Dallas Babb. Bardoe slowly but certainly started to doubt his initial plan. It looked as if Babb could not be goaded into making an appearance, and that no one had the gumption to turn him in for the reward Bardoe offered.

After only a few more minutes of thought, Bardoe decided he'd give it two more days. If Babb didn't show,

Bardoe would do it the hard way. He'd hunt him down just like he hunted down so many men in the past. This time, however, special allowances would not be made in order to take his man before a judge.

****

Martha Henry's heart pounded with the force of a blacksmith's hammer. She hadn't been able to get a good look at his eyes because they were shaded by the stiff brim of his famed hat with the Montana peak, but she certainly felt their power as he stared at her from across the room. Just the force of that glare, that she did not dare return, did things to her body that no man's hands had ever done. This Clay Bardoe certainly presented himself as a grand specimen of the male gender. In that respect, she almost considered it a pity he would die here today.

All those newspaper articles had gotten it correct as far as Martha observed. They all painted a picture of him sitting erect and draped in his dark duster with his back planted squarely in the corner of the room. Martha did not think it common for men to wear their long coats indoors for lengthy periods of time. Most would secure them behind their saddle's cantle. The fact Bardoe had his on, and the fact it had three holes in the back that Martha could not see, magnified the man's ominous presence as if he represented Old Man Death himself sitting in that corner.

Martha fully intended to persuade her Dallas to strip the man of his coat once the deed came to fruition. She could not imagine a more perfect trophy to display, announcing for all to see that she, Martha Henry, had observed in person, the gun battle between Dallas Babb and Clay Bardoe.

Also, just like the papers read, the pearled handled Colts lay at the ready on the table along with the horrible knife that robbed Bardoe of his life mate. Martha paid special attention to how Bardoe's hands rested to the left and right of the array of deadly items.

The hands appeared calm as pond water with the exception of the index finger of Bardoe's right hand, which tapped the table top with a slow but regular rhythm. He seemed to count down the seconds to the moment he would pick up his choice of the killing tools and put them to use.

For Martha, the drumming index finger counted down the seconds before her man would walk through the swinging doors, cross his arms, make his declaration, and then shoot to death the man occupying the far corner of the Drover's Saloon.

Martha, fighting back a smile, counted in unison with the thumping finger.

****

Dallas Babb leaned against the outside wall beside the swinging doors of the Drover's Saloon with his head down so the brim of his hat covered his face. It would not do for someone to recognize him and make an announcement that could only serve to alert his Uncle Clay that the moment of reckoning was at hand.

When finally his mind told his heart enough time had passed, Babb took a deep breath and pushed through the swinging doors. He did not do so in a rush, but with a swagger of confidence... tall and proud. Such an entrance did not go unnoticed. Therefore, neither did his identity. More than one man in the Drover's knew Babb and recognized him in an instant. Without having to say a word, a path like the parting of the Red Sea cleared between where Babb stood and Clay Bardoe sat.

Babb had played out in his head how the moment Bardoe laid eyes on him, he'd all but leap out of that chair he had tucked in the corner – not out of fear, but out of shear surprise. Bardoe hunted down the others, but Babb brought the fight to him. That should have forced Bardoe to his feet... but it didn't. The first glimpse Babb got of his uncle revealed no more than a hard, cold stare and a posture of calm indifference.

The fact Bardoe just sat and glared and didn't twitch a muscle served both to anger Babb and just so slightly unnerve him. He did not appreciate any man, no matter how notorious, to show so little respect for his reputation as a dangerous man. Also, Babb felt a mere tremble in the tips of his fingers. He found it discomforting that Bardoe obviously experienced nothing similar.

Babb's ire and anxiety intertwined to produce a snarl. Bardoe's lack of good sense to be afraid just made it all that much easier for Babb to show him the error of his ways. Babb straightened where he stood, parted his legs to a stalwart stance and folded his arms over his chest.

"Uncle Clay Bardoe," his voice rang out, "you have soiled my reputation... "

****

Clay Bardoe heard tales of fearless men, but he'd never met one. In every occasion as a lawman, in which he'd been faced with or forced to violence, he experienced varying degrees of fear. Sometimes it ached mildly and at other times it struck as nearly suffocating. Being no stranger to the emotion, it now occurred to Bardoe as he eyed his nephew, that fear had been the one thing missing from his dealings with the men who killed his Millie. Every time he'd pulled the knife, or the trigger, or delivered a blow, there had been no room in him for fear. The part of him housing such feelings had been filled to capacity with rage.

That did not now prove to be the case, and the surging of the once familiar emotion puzzled Bardoe. What should he now be afraid of? That Babb would kill him? Bardoe certainly did not dread death. If anything, he longed for it. Neither did the pain of taking bullets worry Bardoe. He'd taken bullets before, three in the back, and he recalled no immediate pain worthy of producing the kind of fear he presently experienced.

Not until the very second that his nephew arrogantly crossed his arms did Bardoe grasp the reason of his substantial anxiety. The fear did not exist over the possibilities of Babb killing or wounding him; he feared Babb besting him, and depriving him of the opportunity to finish his task. And the odds looked damned good that Babb would. In practice, shooting at stationary objects that could not shoot back, Babb proved in the past to be much better than Bardoe. The question to be answered, revolved around how good Babb performed when the lead flew in both directions.

"Uncle Clay Bardoe," the voice boomed, "you have soiled my reputation… "

If this proud and contemptuous young man survived to claim victory in the ensuing contest, Bardoe would die in vain, and the death of his loving wife would go for eternity without being fully revenged. Nothing Bardoe imagined could be more worthy of fearing.

****

Although she thought her anxiety had peaked, Martha Henry's pulse and breath quickened even more when her man took his stance and started bringing his arms up to cross over his chest. Martha seemed to view it all in slow motion. Her eyes darted between Babb and Bardoe. Her own hands trembled in anticipation and she could not fathom how either of these men displayed no sign of the trepidation they must have felt. Both appeared steady as stone and as cool as a late autumn breeze.

As she imagined this event in her mind the past few days, which she'd done countless times, she pictured both men standing and facing off as depicted in the dime novels. It surprised her that Bardoe remained in his chair and showed no signs of coming to his feet. Martha made sure to study Bardoe's face the moment Babb stepped through the swinging doors. To her amazement, Bardoe reacted only by pushing the hat back further on his head. Only then did she observe a slight widening of the lids housing his cold blue eyes.

Even now, as Babb brought his arms up just like he said he would, Bardoe's index finger continued to slowly and solemnly thump on the table before him. The patrons who scurried well away from the anticipated line of fire fell silent as church mice. The only sound to be heard was the almost booming thump of the finger on the table counting down the moments until it would thump no more.

Babb's arms folded into place, and Martha smiled in anticipation of the words, and then the action to follow.

"Uncle Clay Bardoe," her Dallas announced in a voice that reverberated with pride and confidence, "you have soiled my reputation… "

Martha tore her eyes from Babb to quickly look to Bardoe for a reaction.

The finger stopped thumping.

Babb paused to let his words sink in and then opened his mouth to say the rest, when Bardoe folded his right hand on the closest of the .45's, quickly brought it up, and fired a single shot.

Time did actually stand still for Martha Henry. It might have been, she believed, that her heart for a moment ceased to beat. The roaring sound of the single shot seemed to tumble over and over in her ears like thunder rolling across the prairie. Without thinking, she jumped to her feet and padded toward her man. Dallas Babb lay on his back. The hole in his forehead left him not even enough of life's energy to twitch. Martha stared down into wide open eyes that seemed to express, even in death, a great deal of surprise.

****

The female stranger slipped Bardoe's mind until he saw her rushing toward Babb's corpse. He watched curiously as she stared down at the freshly dead outlaw. Although she shed no tears, it looked as if there had been a relationship. Bardoe deduced that Babb brought her along from somewhere to observe an event he surely believed would turn out somewhat differently.

After a few moments, the woman turned from Babb to stare at Bardoe. He could not decipher the look on her face. The handsome woman seemed to be feeling something between sadness and curiosity. After only a brief hesitation, she started toward Bardoe in a deliberate fashion and did not falter before reaching his table.

"He had more words to say, and then he was going to kill you," the woman stated as a simple matter of fact that surprisingly held no contempt.

Bardoe looked the woman square in the eye for long seconds before replying, "There is a time for talking and a time for killing. I guess the boy got the two times confused."

"How does it feel to have shot dead your very own nephew?" The woman asked in a manner that did not seem the least bit accusatory, but wholly inquisitive.

It was a good question that Bardoe had not yet enough time to ponder. Now, he took a few minutes of silence to do just that while the woman stood patiently and seemed to study him.

When the answer came to Bardoe, he shared it with the woman whose name he didn't care to know. "When Dallas was just a young boy, I taught him a trade I thought he might use to follow in what was then my footsteps. Years later it became all too apparent to me that he was, after all, his father's son. It simply was not in him to do good, and I regretted teaching him all I had.

"When his evil ways led to the death of my dear wife, I no longer looked upon him as kin. I have no regrets for what I did here today. May his soul burn in hell."

"You are a hard man," the woman said with a strange hint of appreciation.

"What was he to you?" Bardoe asked, giving in to his curiosity.

"I took him to my bed a short while ago," the woman replied with a wisp of a smile. "And now, I find myself wanting to do the same with you."

Bardoe pushed to his feet and stared down on the smiling woman. "I find you despicable. Leave this place now, or I will put a bullet between your eyes as well."

The smile dissolved instantly and a grimace grew in its place. "The now famed Clay Bardoe would murder an unarmed lady in cold blood?"

"Woman," Bardoe snarled, "you wouldn't make a fair-sized wart on a real lady's ass. Go now... and that is your final warning."

The woman threw her chin in the air and turned and walked away without another word. She swished right past the body of Dallas Babb without bothering to pay him even a final glance.

****

Bardoe sat and calmly sipped whiskey as he watched Sid Rowden and an assistant drag Babb's body out the front doors of the Drover's Saloon.

The only comment he cared to make was, "Drop his valuables off at his mama's house, Sid."

He sipped even more whiskey as he watched the bartender Rusty Gains mop up the blood that spouted from Babb's head. He grew more talkative as Gains went about his task.

"I'm guessing, Rusty, that you are well pleased that my business here is now concluded."

"Your business has been good for my business, Mr. Bardoe. I'm in no hurry to see you depart," Gains said with a sincere tone as he looked up from the gory mess.

"Well, it's time for me to be moving on."

An hour passed, and Bardoe found himself without a clue as to where he'd be moving on to. He struggled with thoughts of options he could consider when Avery Jinks from the telegraph office popped in through the swinging doors.

"Got a telegraph for you, Mr. Bardoe," Jinks croaked from a place right inside the door. The tall and thin Jinks had a reputation of being habitually nervous.

"Well, you going to bring it to me, Avery, or are you going to make me get up and come over there and get it?"

"Why, shoot fire, Mr. Bardoe, I wasn't about to approach that table without permission to do so," Jinks nodded like a tom turkey.

"Avery, you have no reason to fear me. Bring me what you got."

Jinks still stopped far enough away that he had to stretch to hand Bardoe his message.

Bardoe read the words once, took a shot of whiskey, and then read them a second time.

"Will you be wanting to return a message?" Jinks asked.

"It don't demand a response," Bardoe grumbled.

Avery Jinks disappeared in a flash.

The words of the message had been few and clear in meaning: "You are wanted in Guthrie for the murder of the prostitute Jenny Mills. I'll be coming to serve the warrant."

CB Wooly was coming, and Bardoe responded by waiving Rusty Gains over to his table.

At least Gains would be pleased. If Bardoe chose to leave, he'd have to do so quickly, and he would be forced to scurry to a place as far away as Mexico or Canada. Truthfully, Bardoe surmised, he simply did not possess the desire to either hurry or scurry. In only seconds he made up his mind to occupy his corner table a day or two longer.

"You might pass this around, Rusty. A show like this could draw a passel of thirsty onlookers," Bardoe said as he handed the telegraph Gains.

The bartender took long moments to read the message. "You plan to just sit and wait for CB Wooly to show up?" Rusty asked with eyes nearly at the bugging stage.

"I ain't much at running. Even if I was, CB Wooly is a damned hard man to escape."

"Are you going to let him take you in, Mr. Bardoe?"

"Most likely not."

Rusty Gains had his lips posed for another question when the sound of heavily hit swinging doors banged against the inner front walls and reverberated throughout the saloon. Someone just entered the Drover's in a fast and furious manner.

Instinctively, the bartender jumped clear of the seated man, clearing Bardoe's field of vision. A plump woman with graying hair and a Colt 1851 Navy Revolver in each hand stomped towards Bardoe.

"You killed my boy!" Lyle Babb screamed through the tears and spittle covering her beet-red face. "Now I will kill you!"

Bardoe leaned back in his chair until the two front legs lifted off the ground. He brought his arms across his chest and simply waited for his sister to cover the few remaining yards separating them.

Lyle had only feet to go when she brought both guns up shoulder high and cocked both hammers. Bardoe did not twitch a muscle. Had the table not stopped her, Lyle would have probably borne down even closer to the seated man. Up against the table with her arms extended, Lyle thrust both barrels of the Colts only inches from Bardoe's body.

"Are you prepared to meet your maker?" she screamed in near hysterics.

Bardoe's left arm remained folded over his right but he slowly lifted his left hand and used his index finger to point to a place in the middle of his chest.

"Point them both right here, Lyle, and blaze away."

Lyle Babb bellowed and she stomped and she blew tears and spit, but she did not pull either trigger. Then she dropped her head and the guns, and stood and wailed. Bardoe folded the left hand back into the cradle of his right arm and did nothing to comfort his sister. There remained no comfort left in him to give.

When she seemed to cry herself out, Lyle raised her head and said, "I can't do it. You are all the family I have left."

Bardoe nodded his head and sighed, "That is a true pity, Lyle... on both accounts."

After his sister stumbled from the Drover's, Bardoe looked to Rusty Gains as he climbed from beneath a nearby table.

"Rusty, I'll need two bottles to take up to my room.

Should CB Wooly show before I've recovered from my drunken state, please ask him to take his leave until I've sobered."

CHAPTER TWELVE

No Chance in Hell

The Mosier place sat not too far out of CB Wooly's way. For reasons he did not fully want to understand, he felt a need to pay a visit to the brothers' graves.

The day had quickly grown old and the sun was not long from setting. Wooly planned on paying his respects and then picking a place to camp overnight somewhere between the Mosier farm and Stillwater.

He crested a small knoll to find himself looking down on a cabin and barnyard. He encountered no difficulty locating the four graves from that vantage point. It proved a simple task made even simpler by the two figures standing side by side and centered on the row of graves. Wooly visited this homestead once before shortly after the warrants had been issued for the Mosier boys. The two people could only be the two remaining members of the Mosier clan.

Wooly rode in at a wide arc so the Mosiers could spot him long before his arrival. A straight in approach would have put him at their backs and the two old people would not have had enough time, if their mourning made it necessary, to compose themselves. He removed his hat and stopped at a respectable distance from the mounds of bare earth.

He nodded a solemn greeting before saying, "I am sorry for you folks' loss."

Old man Mosier nodded back in response, but said not a thing. The old lady did the talking.

"That day you came looking for them, I wished they'd been here, Marshal Wooly."

"Ma'am, I do too. I surely do."

"I wish a lot of things," Mother Mosier said before pointing a finger – bent and crooked from years of hard work – at the third mound in the line of four. "That's where my oldest lies. I knew well before his tenth year that he bore no good. It's hard for a mother to say, but I wish back then I'd a taken him out in the woods someplace and left him. If I had, my other three would be alive today. I'd trade one for three. Especially if the one I had to trade was Leroy."

"That boy… " Father Mosier inserted, "… just wasn't right in neither the head… nor the heart."

The old man never uttered a word in Wooly's presence before now, and he doubted he'd ever hear another because it seemed Mr. Mosier just said all he intended to say. Not so with his wife.

"Are you in these parts looking for that rotten bastard Dallas Babb?" Mother Mosier asked.

"Well, ma'am, if I was to stumble upon him, I'd sure take holt of him. But the honest truth is, I'm headed to Stillwater to bring in Clay Bardoe for killing a woman."

Wooly's statement clearly filled Mother Mosier's head with all kinds of thoughts and it took her seconds to apparently sort them out.

"I reckon that would be the whore that died with my Leroy. That boy never had the good sense to find him a decent woman."

Wooly shrugged and nodded.

"Now, for that Clay Bardoe, I have a conflict of feelings. I can't say he didn't have a right to avenge his wife's death. Yet, I do hold against him how he dispensed his revenge on Leroy. No mama wants to see a son die so badly, no matter how deserving that son might have been. Yet again, I am thankful Clay Bardoe did not let my Bob suffer any more than he was already suffering. I ain't but sure that he did not do Bob a great favor by putting a bullet in his head. Bob was nothing like his brother Leroy."

Wooly nodded and shrugged and shrugged and nodded throughout the oration.

"And as for you, Marshal Wooly, you strike me as a good and decent man. For that reason I feel obliged to tell you I suddenly feel in my heart that you should leave Clay Bardoe be. Heed my words and turn your horse in another direction."

Wooly allowed himself a grimace before replying, "I just can't do that, Missus Mosier."

Mother Mosier studied him hard for a minute or maybe two before nodding her head and coming as close to smiling as she seemed capable. "I wish I'd had a son like you. I bet your ma is awfully proud of the man you become."

"I think she was pleased, ma'am," Wooly sighed, "but she passed on to her place in glory a short while back."

Mother Mosier pursed her lips and glanced across the line of graves before looking back up at Wooly. "Well, you have no ma and I have no more boys. If you'd allow, it would do my heart good to fix you a bite to eat before you head on your way."

Wooly nodded again but this time he smiled instead of shrugging. "I'd be much obliged, Missus Mosier."

****

Wooly made it about halfway between the Mosier farm and Stillwater before nightfall. He gazed intently into his campfire when first his tethered horse snorted and then whinnied. When another horse returned a like response from close by, Wooly removed his pistol from his holster and held it down alongside his leg.

"Hello there," a peaceful enough voice called from the dark. "Can I join you at your fire?"

Wooly stood and faced the direction from whence the voice had come and called back, "Come on in."

Wooly could hear the creaking that leather made when a rider shifted his weight from the seat of the saddle to the left stirrup in order to dismount. Seconds later a fairly short but stoutly built man with a large black hat bearing a large crease down the middle, led his horse into the dancing light thrown off by the fire.

It took Wooly a few seconds to call a name, but he recognized the man immediately. "Floyd Danner... I thought you'd still be in prison."

Danner cocked his head and squinted his eyelids until his eyes adjusted to the light. Once he could see, it didn't take him any longer to recognize Wooly than it had Wooly to recognize him. "Marshal CB Wooly? Damnation! I don't think I'd be any more surprised had I ran across a naked lady out here! A hell of a lot happier, but no more surprised," Danner exclaimed with a wide grin.

"Did you bust out of that Texas prison, Floyd?" Wooly asked while intentionally turning to reveal the gun held down alongside his leg.

Danner stared at the gun a second or two before looking back up and into Wooly's face. "Hell, no, CB, I did my time. I was in that God-awful stink hole for five long years and have been out for three. And you can put that cannon you carry back in the holster. I ain't been in no more trouble these three years, and you know good and well I was never the type to harm a man of the law anyway."

Wooly dubbed the statement true enough and put his gun away, but couldn't help but chuckle at a memory. "You obviously were never the type meant to hold up stagecoaches either."

Danner shook his head and laughed right along with Wooly. "Didn't that beat all? My first damned stage robbery, and I was so drunk I passed out at the scene of my own crime! I had all the loot tucked away, then I just fell out of the saddle and laid on the ground like a warm lump of shit!"

Danner's response had Wooly laughing even harder. "I must have known back then, but I've forgotten now... what possessed you to hold up a stage in such an advanced state of inebriation?"

"Why, hell, CB, I was never no outlaw. So when I decided to try my hand at it that one and only time, I turned as nervous as a plump dog at a pow-wow! I got to that place in the road where I intended to rob the stage about three hours too early. There happened a bottle of whiskey in my saddle bag and I drank the entire damned thing. It took me four attempts to just get on my horse after I drank it. Hell, I shoulda known I couldn't of stayed in the saddle!"

Wooly still laughed as he said, "I got to admit, you was sure enough the easiest to catch highwayman I ever took to jail, and the most pleasant to boot. I remember now how once you sobered up, you kept me and ol' Clay Bardoe in stitches all the way to Fort Smith."

Danner scrunched his face. "Now there's a man who has caused me grief a second time since taking me to jail all those years ago."

"Clay Bardoe?" Wooly asked.

"The one and only."

Wooly motioned to the pot on the fire and a log beside the fire. "Grab your cup if you want some coffee, have a seat, and tell me about it."

Danner tethered his horse beside Wooly's before taking a tin cup from the bedroll strapped behind his cantle. After easing down on the log, he poured himself some coffee and began to talk.

"After I got out of prison, I turned to bounty hunting for a living, and I've done fairly well with it. Actually, I'm pretty damned good at it. Once the Mosier boys and Dallas Babb hit that bank up north, I started looking for them. I'll be damned if I wasn't on their trail and not but ten miles east of their hideout when Babb killed those youngest two Mosiers.

"Then I was getting pretty close to running down Leroy and Bob when they did that terribly awful thing to Mrs. Bardoe. Well, after that, Clay started killing them, and I lost out on the Mosiers. So I turned my efforts toward catching Dallas Babb. Just recently I learned he was up in Wichita, but was more than likely headed back this way. Then I'll be damned if Bardoe didn't up and kill him, too."

Wooly straightened and narrowed his eyes. "Bardoe killed Babb?"

"Killed him deader than a steer's pecker the day before yesterday at the Drover's Saloon in Stillwater. I wasn't there, but I hear young Babb stomped right into the Drover's and called Bardoe out. Bardoe didn't even get out of his chair. Just picked up one of his guns and made Babb a new hole for a third eye-ball right betwixt his old eye-balls."

Wooly emitted an involuntary sigh and dropped his eyes to stare again into the flames.

"This news seems to distress you, CB," Danner said.

Wooly would not usually tell an uninterested party his business, but at this moment he felt a need to share. "I'm on my way to Stillwater to arrest Clay Bardoe. I don't expect he'll come peacefully. If Babb would have killed my good friend, that would have just kept Clay and me from having to do harm to one another."

Danner sucked on a tooth for a few seconds before saying, "I'm not sure how to put this, CB, because I don't want to offend you… but if it comes to shooting between you and Bardoe, I don't think you have to worry about causing him harm."

"Are you saying, Floyd, that you don't think I could take Clay in a fight with guns?"

"I'm saying you got no chance in hell of winning a shooting match with Bardoe. Does that surprise you, CB?"

"Nope. I just wanted to know if anybody else was seeing it the same as me."

****

Wooly and Floyd Danner rose early the next morning and mounted to ride as the sun popped over the horizon.

"Marshal Wooly, thanks for sharing your campsite. I never held it against you for putting me in jail. Hell, I had no one to blame for that except me. I've often thought it would be a pleasure meeting up with you again, and it damned sure has been." Danner leaned to offer Wooly his right hand.

Wooly shook the hand and respected Danner's powerful grip – which was a mark of something good in a man. "I remember thinking at the time I took you to jail, that if the times and situations were different, we'd probably get along just fine."

"And here we are doing just that, CB. As a matter of fact, only two things keep me from riding with you right now to take on Clay Bardoe. Number one, instead of just killing you, he'd kill us both. Number two, I don't think you'd let me go with you even if I didn't object to dying."

CB shook his head and chuckled. "I don't know why I think that's funny. I ain't too keen on death my ownself. Still, though, you are right. I couldn't take help along to do this job."

Floyd Danner nodded his understanding before saying, "Well, I know you won't consider this either, but I don't want to look back someday, like tomorrow, and think I didn't do all I could to keep you from riding into Stillwater.

"I'm headed out to the New Mexico and Arizona territories. Believe it or not, I'm going to try my hand at law work. I hear there are small towns out that way willing to pay handsome sums to have the rowdies cleared from their domain. I'd like to extend an invitation for you to ride with me."

Wooly had grown fond of Danner in the few hours they'd been together and he expressed his fondness in a smile. "Don't think I'm not tempted, but it don't matter how much money a man has if that man can't live with himself. Guess I'd better ride on into Stillwater."

The two men shook hands once more before Danner reined his horse toward the west. He hadn't gone far before turning in the saddle and calling back, "CB Wooly, I hope you live to see another sunrise."

Wooly hoped for the same.

CHAPTER THIRTEEN

There Will Be Shooting

Bardoe shot up in his bed feeling sick to his stomach. Not from the whiskey, although the room still had a slight spin to it. He felt sick, both in a physical and emotional way, because of a dream. It had felt so real, and still did.

In the dream Bardoe had been at his far corner table in the Drover's. Only two others occupied the bar and both sat at far away tables in two opposing corners. Elvin Timms, the dirty back shooting son of a bitch, sat on Bardoe's left. On his right, far out of his reach, sat Millicent. Elvin Timms still had his face that CB Wooly long ago took off with the double-barrel shotgun, and Millicent appeared as beautiful as ever... the way she looked before those now dead tore her asunder.

Bardoe could not move and he could not speak because Millie told him CB was coming, and Timms said, "You'll have to kill him, Bardoe."

Millie pleaded with Clay not to take the life of his oldest friend. Bardoe wanted to respond, but his lips and his tongue simply would not work. Millie did not understand why Bardoe could not respond to her words. "If you love me as much as I know you do, Clay Bardoe, you will not lift a hand against CB."

"If you don't," Timms laughed, "then you will either swing from a rope or spend the rest of your days in some dark and filthy prison."

"If you kill him, Clay," Millie countered, "you will not spend eternity with me."

Millicent and Timms continued to tug at both Bardoe's conscience and will to survive until CB Wooly walked through the swinging doors.

CB had his gun in hand, and instinctively, Bardoe picked both of his up from the table top. CB fired once and missed. Bardoe returned fire… once, twice, and a third time… and he did not miss. Without as much as a thought, Bardoe put three bullets in CB Wooly's chest. CB took such a terribly long time to die.

While CB lay on the floor and gasped and kicked and moaned and called the name of his dead mother, Timms bellowed with laughter, and Millicent sobbed uncontrollably.

Slowly and surely, Millie dissolved away into a mist. Bardoe remained for what was obviously an eternity, watching Wooly slowly and painfully die while Elvin Timms found it all so terribly funny.

Now Bardoe remained in his bed hoping the sick feeling would subside. When it didn't, he struggled to stand and slowly started to dress. He feared this day to be, just one of many to follow, that he did not want to live. In his heart, though, he knew this day would stand out from the others because it would be the day he found himself forced to kill CB Wooly.

****

At a few minutes shy of ten a.m., CB Wooly took a deep breath, pushed through the swinging doors, and walked into the Drover's Saloon. The table in the far rear corner sat vacant, and CB exhaled his breath. Only a few serious drinkers inhabited the place and they paid CB no mind. The bartender worked steadily at his place behind the bar.

"Bar keep," Wooly nodded as he approached, "I'm here in search of Clay Bardoe."

The bartender, a fairly big guy with a ruddy complexion, seemed to gulp in more than his share of air. "You are Marshal CB Wooly," he sputtered.

"That I am. Can I find Clay on these premises?"

"Marshal, sir, I have a message from Mr. Bardoe for you."

"Give it."

"He is at this moment, I'm sure, recovering from several bottles of whiskey, and he has requested that you take your leave until he sends word that he is in a more agreeable state."

Despite his heavy heart, Wooly could not help but grin. "I'll post myself in the city marshal's office. I'll give Clay until three today to become more agreeable."

Wooly glanced back at the table in the far corner and studied it several seconds before turning to leave. He made it nearly to the front doors when his eyes fell upon a wide and dark spot on the roughhewn planks of the floor. Wooly looked back to the bartender and questioned, "Dallas Babb?"

"Dallas Babb," the bartender nodded.

Wooly looked from the floor to the far table. "That's a good fifty paces."

"Yes sir, at least. And Mr. Bardoe drilled him square between the eyes with his one and only shot."

Wooly rubbed at the back of his neck a second before turning and again starting on his way. The bartender stopped him this time.

"Marshal Wooly?"

Wooly turned. "Yup?"

The big man suddenly looked all kinds of uncomfortable. "I have a favor to ask of you, and it's... well... unpleasant."

"You can ask it."

The bartender nodded his head and cleared his throat twice. "If you come back here to confront Mr. Bardoe, could you make your stand to either the far right or far left of Babb's stain?"

Wooly knew exactly what the man insinuated and why, but just for grins, he cocked his head and expressed confusion. Levity might just ease his mood and it would be fun seeing the man fumble over his reasoning.

"Uh, well... you see, Marshal, that stain has already brought in a slew of customers. Uh... " The bartender paused to clear his throat and then cough a couple of times. "... the truth is... two stains ought to bring in twice as many customers."

Wooly shook his head in disbelief, but couldn't help but smile as he did so.

"Tell you what, barkeep, should it come down to my bleeding, I'll do my damnedest to bleed in a different spot."

****

Rusty Gains found himself damned busy by noon. The word that CB Wooly had come to town spread like spilled milk on a table top. It seemed everyone thought they wanted a front row seat to what couldn't help but be a tie for the greatest gun battle to ever take place in Stillwater.

Gains stayed busy, but not too busy to look up from behind the bar to the top of the stairs about every other minute. It just so happened, at a minute he wasn't looking, Clay Bardoe stepped into view on the second floor landing. Gains detected the fact by the sudden and practically absolute silence that fell over the busy tavern. He jerked his head to look up and find the slender figure – complete in all his now famed clothing and gear – scowling down at the packed room.

The talent of reading people like books stood as a key characteristic of every good bartender. Although it had been one of his greatest challenges, Gains had learned to read

Bardoe fairly well over the past weeks. Clearly, Bardoe took no pleasure from all the fanfare.

His displeasure emanated so distinctly in fact, that the throng of on-lookers picked up on it as well. Those at the bottom of the stairs began finding another place to be, and all those looking up to the landing turned their eyes on other things. In an obvious release of nervous energy, voices picked up in volume, discussing anything out loud except the man standing at the top of the stairs. No single person in the Drover's wanted to attract Bardoe's attention.

Few, other than Gains, stared directly at Bardoe as he made his way down the stairs with his left arm down along his side and the palm of his right hand resting on the handle of the knife protruding from the front of his gun belts. Gains had watched Bardoe descend the same stairs on a good number of mornings. On this particular one he moved much slower than usual.

A path cleared as Bardoe made his way to the bar. A close-up view of Bardoe's face shocked Gains. He bore the look of a person with a bad illness. In his line of business, Gains had viewed more people than he could count who'd been badly affected by too many hours of drinking too much hard liquor. Although Gains could not accurately diagnose

Bardoe's problem, he knew it was no hangover plaguing the man.

"Wooly's in town," Bardoe declared the obvious. "What else could draw such a crowd?"

"Yes sir, Mr. Bardoe, he's waiting at the town marshal's office for word from you."

"I'd like you to do me two favors," Bardoe said with no enthusiasm whatsoever. "I'd like you to send someone for CB, and I'd like you to close your business for the short time it will take to conclude this matter."

"Yes sir, I can do both. No sense in taking a chance of innocent people getting hit."

Bardoe slowly surveyed the room before muttering, "There are no innocent people in here."

****

Bardoe leaned against the bar while waiting alone in the cavernous saloon. Five minutes earlier he watched a disgruntled crowd funnel out the swinging doors. However, it turned out that no one felt so disgruntled as to bring it directly to his attention. Bardoe now moved from the bar to his corner table. It surprised him how much louder boot heels on plank floors sounded in an empty building. The jingling of his spurs seemed to echo all around him.

Bardoe stood near his chair and pulled both of his pearl handled Colts, butts first, and laid them out on the table with the barrels facing the swinging doors. He removed the Bowie knife from his belt with his right hand, placing the blade flat in the palm of his left hand. For several seconds he studied the knife, while a legion of bad memories and feelings seemed to pierce his heart. When he could stand it not a moment longer, he brought the knife up high and drove it downward with enough force to bury several inches of its blade into the table top between the two pistols. No matter what happened this day, he knew he would never touch this terrible knife again.

Before taking a seat, Bardoe removed his duster, folded it in half and draped it across the back of a nearby chair. He'd worn it as a warning for those he sought, that it would take a force from hell to kill Clay Bardoe. CB Wooly wouldn't need that warning. Bardoe pulled back his chair and settled down into it to watch the swinging doors. All that remained was a short wait.

****

Rusty Gains all but burst through the door of the city marshal's office and came near to getting his ass shot by Marshal Gray Wilson.

Wooly thought that as jumpy as Wilson seemed, one might think it was his responsibility to soon serve a warrant on Clay Bardoe. That somewhat irritated Wooly. The look on the face of the bartender, along with his overall demeanor, irritated him as well. You'd have thought the man a virgin groom, only minutes away from consummating his marriage.

"He's ready for you!" Gains boomed with too much exuberance.

"You are having a high time with this, ain't you?" Wooly scowled.

Gains evidently possessed some skill at reading scowls because he instantly grew sober. "I mean no offense, Marshal Wooly, but this kind of thing don't happen every day."

"What kind of thing?" Wooly shot back.

"A shooting thing between two men of notoriety that were once the best of friends."

"Who says there is going to be shooting? He might just let me arrest him," Wooly hissed. The whole situation had him suddenly feeling mean.

Gains took on a puzzled look as if he'd never considered any outcome other than another stain on his plank floors. That look quickly disappeared when Gray Wilson spouted off.

"Oh, there will be shooting, CB. I guarantee there will be shooting."

Wooly found his mouth ready to spout profanities, but then he paused to take a few deep breaths. Who was he trying to fool? Of course there would be shooting. Shouting for Gray Wilson to kiss his saddle-flattened ass wasn't going to change that. Wooly turned and walked out the door without another word to the petty city marshal or the giddy bartender.

Wooly became all out flabbergasted by the number of people lining the streets and sidewalks. He let it be known by his stride and facial expressions that they best stay clear of his path. Hell, it looked like a circus had come to town... and featured Wooly as its death defying act.

****

Bardoe could tell by the escalating roar of the crowd out in the streets that CB Wooly drew near. He momentarily dropped his eyes to stare at the pistols positioned at the ready, before settling back in his chair and training his eyes on the swinging doors.

Wooly showed no hesitation. He strode through the doors and right up to Bardoe's table. He reached out and grabbed a chair from the closest table, swung it around backwards and then straddled it. Wooly leaned forward and folded his arms across the back of the chair. Then he smiled that old familiar smile.

"We have found ourselves a many a times in a terrible fix, old friend," he said. "But this time we have a sure-fired doozy on our hands."

"It's a doozy, all right," Bardoe replied. Despite himself he could not help but return the friendly smile.

"Do you remember that time we were looking for old Jesse and Frank and the boys up there in the Sansbois mountains, when my horse just walked off the side of that cliff?"

Just two minutes earlier the farthest thing from Bardoe's mind was laughter. Now, he was helpless to do anything but chuckle. "That would be hard to forget, CB."

"To this day I cannot figure what would make a damned good and sure-footed animal just waltz off the side of a mountain. One minute I was in the saddle on solid ground, and the next I'm still in the saddle but dropping like a rock through the sky. I remember tugging on the reins to beat all hell...like that was going to change a damned thing. Me and that old horse are flying through the air and I'm hollering at the top of my lungs, 'Whoa! Whoa, damn you! Whoa!'"

In his mind's eye Bardoe could picture, like he had many times, CB Wooly and the horse dropping from the sky and ol' CB pulling on the reins with all his might. For the first time since the morning he'd warned Millicent about the snakes, Bardoe laughed hard.

"Silly as it may sound," Wooly continued, "I kept looking down and seeing that rocky floor coming up fast and the only damned plan I could come up with was that I'd wait till the last second... just before my horse plowed into the earth... and then I'd simply swing out of the saddle and step easily to the ground.

"Then all of a sudden, like a hand reaching out from heaven, there was that sturdy oak growing out of the side of the mountain. I turned my head to the left and there it was, and I just simply reached out and grabbed a stout branch with both hands. And there I dangled until you threw down a rope."

Wooly just sat and looked on with a smile while Bardoe finished his laughter. Bardoe had it down to a mere snicker when Wooly swung back out of his chair and walked over behind the bar to grab a bottle of whiskey and two glasses.

"One of us will later need to settle up with the saloon keeper for this," Wooly grinned as he threw a leg back over the chair and sat down to pour two glasses of the whiskey. He picked up his and held it toward Bardoe.

"To the old times."

Bardoe held his glass in the air and nodded his agreement before both men downed the honey colored elixir. Then the look on Wooly's face just went serious.

"Clay, are you going to allow me to take you into my custody and escort you to Guthrie?"

Three minutes earlier Bardoe would have presented his answer both hard and fast, but at the moment, he found himself wavering – a sin he seldom committed. This time he picked up the bottle and filled the glasses. He took his glass to his lips and downed it again.

"CB, I'd like to take five minutes to consider your question. I'd ask you to wait outside while I do so."

Wooly nodded his understanding as he pushed to his feet. When standing, he picked up his glass and gulped down the whiskey. He put it back down, then extended his right hand down to Bardoe.

"However this may go, I've never had a better friend," Wooly said solemnly.

Bardoe took the hand and both men shook with conviction. "I can and do say the same."

Bardoe let Wooly get almost to the doors.

"CB," he called.

Wooly executed a half turn. "Yup, Clay?"

"I didn't flat-out murder that whore."

"I didn't expect you did."

"She had Leroy Mosier's gun. She shot once and was ready to shoot a second time. Bob Mosier and Dallas Babb still had to pay."

"I would reckon, Clay, that you'd have a good chance in front of a jury."

"As long as you believe what I'm saying, CB, a jury can be damned."

"You might have turned to killing, Clay, but I'd whip any man's ass if they's ever to call you a liar."

****

The slatted double-swinging doors of the Drover's Saloon were of the full-size, floor to ceiling variation. Had they been the kind that hit an average sized man at about the chest and knees, Wooly would most likely view a gaggle of leering faces and a tangle of arms and legs jockeying for position as he walked away from Bardoe's table. With the Drover's doors concealing his view, he could only assume that such nonsense thrived on the other side, so on his way out, he hit them hard in hopes of banging some of the heads that were no doubt pressed to the slats in order to hear what transpired on the inside. It felt good to do so, because not so deep down inside himself, Wooly struggled with an awfully dark mood. The fact also did not escape him, that the large crowd milling outside the Drover's had come to see a killing, and the greatest majority of them thought Wooly not long for this world.

As hoped for, a cacophony of howls and bellows sounded as Wooly plowed through the doors. Two of the eavesdroppers tumbled to the ground and a good half dozen others staggered backwards holding or rubbing body parts that had connected with the doors. Although he moved the wall of people back a few feet, Wooly barely had enough room to stand on the wooden walk outside the saloon.

Because he needed more space and would welcome any opportunity to let off some steam, Wooly pulled his gun and hollered, "If I can reach anyone of you with this pistol from where I stand, I will club you over the head until you fall to your knees!"

He felt more than a little disappointment when the threatened quickly moved far out of his reach. Some moved back so far that Wooly was able to lay eyes on a sight that truly astounded him.

The crowd had consisted mostly of men – cowboys, ruffians, gamblers, a few of the local business owners – even a few whores. But in the street only a few yards away was a fancy Heiss buggy, which held a lovely and dignified lady, who Wooly would guess was no stranger to wealth and high living. Yet, here she sat among mostly the low life, obviously anxiously awaiting blood to be shed. Wooly turned his head from the buggy in disgust.

He'd been so intent on breaking body parts with the door that he failed to check the time on his pocket watch. It didn't really matter though. When Wooly figured it time to go back in, he'd just go back in. Bardoe would not be shy about asking for additional time if he had underestimated the time passed, and he probably would not give a damn if Wooly went long by a minute or two either.

Just as Wooly decided that enough time had passed, a disturbance among the gathering caught his attention. The people in the crowd abruptly split to the right and left as someone barreled his way toward Wooly. In a matter of seconds the large black hat with the middle crease came into Wooly's view.

The man beneath the hat stood shorter than most in the crowd, but was strong enough that no man yet had barred his way.

Floyd Danner, breathing hard from his effort of pushing and shoving, stepped up on the plank walk beside Wooly and flashed a beaming smile.

"You sure know how to draw an audience, Marshal Wooly."

"I thought you was headed west," Wooly managed to smile.

"Oh, hell, I hear the west has been out that way a long time. It'll probably wait around another couple more days for me. Besides, my conscience got to bothering me. Thought I best find you and lend a hand anyway I could."

Just the mere fact that Wooly had someone standing beside him did a world of good for his innards. He relayed to Danner why he was occupying the boardwalk instead of being inside shooting it out with Bardoe.

"I can't allow you to go in there with me. It's one of those damned things a man just has to do all by his lonesome," Wooly sighed. "Yet, if and when you hear shooting, I'd appreciate it if you'd stand here and keep these vultures from swooping in. If I'm the one shot, I don't want them picking me clean for souvenirs. If I get damned lucky, I'll need a moment of peace to consider what I've done to my old partner."

"I can keep them out," Danner nodded.

Wooly nodded his belief that the man in fact could.

"Well, guess I'll mosey on in."

"If the shooting starts," Danner said as he placed a hand on Wooly's shoulder, "once it's stopped, will you holler out and let me know if you're still standing?"

"If I'm still standing... I'll damn sure holler."

CHAPTER FOURTEEN

Made Me Kill You

W ooly stepped through the doors and could tell instantly by the expression on Bardoe's face that he did not intend to be placed under arrest. The expression stopped Wooly in his tracks.

"We going to do it the hard way, aren't we, Clay?"

Wooly watched as Bardoe inhaled a very deep breath and let it out slowly. "I can't take a chance on some jury finding me guilty. A prison term or even a sentence to hang just would not do for me. Being locked away in prison, for a man like me, would be hell on earth and you know it, CB. It would be much worse than hanging. But hanging...well hanging is such an undignified way to leave this life. And years from now, most of all I ever did... good and bad... would be forgotten, and I'd just be known as a man who hung by the neck for killing a woman."

Wooly sincerely wished he could tell Bardoe he was wrong, but he wasn't. Wooly took his own deep breath and let it out slowly.

"CB."

"Yup?"

"Pull your pistol, cock it and point it. You got the first shot."

"Clay," Wooly warned, "you know I'm a different kind of man than Walt Tabor. I won't dance this dance like he did."

"You think I don't know that, CB?"

Wooly took a few seconds to make a point of slowly looking around the large room.

"Clay, I don't see no stout oak branches for me to grab onto this time. Do you?"

Bardoe let a few seconds pass before shaking his head.

"Nope."

Wooly raised his right hand and showed his palm to Bardoe before slowly moving it down to his holstered gun. He pulled it, cocked it, took aim... and pulled the trigger.

"DAMN!" Wooly shouted when his single shot sent plaster dust and particles flying from the wall not an inch left of Bardoe's right ear. He'd aimed for his old friend's chest.

Wooly barely had the word out of his mouth before Bardoe's hands wrapped around the pearl handles and the big Colts came up fast. The marshal took aim for a second shot as Bardoe pulled back both hammers. The eight clicks, four from each pistol, sounded clearly in the quiet room. Bardoe didn't aim. He didn't have to. Wooly pulled his trigger a second time.

The big bullet collided in the exact spot where Bardoe's heart pounded and the impact of the round shoved him back against the wall. The front two legs of the chair remained off the ground. The two Colt .45's fell from his hands and clanked loudly as they hit the plank floor. Bardoe's head drooped to rest on his chest, and his light colored Stetson with the razor-sharp brim fell forward to cover his face.

"Damn," Wooly said again, but this time in a whisper.

"CB Wooly?" Floyd Danner's voice sounded from beyond the swinging doors. "Are you alive or dead?"

It took Wooly a second or two to find his speaking voice. "I ain't dead," he hollered back.

****

Danner couldn't help but jump when the first shot went off in the saloon. It couldn't have been more than a heartbeat later before the second one sounded. Then all hell broke loose for Danner.

Three men out in front of a bunch more tried to storm the swinging doors. Danner instinctively pulled his pistol at the sound of the first shot. He clubbed one of the three on the right side of the head while wrapping his left hand around a second man's throat. He choked the man to the ground while kicking the third man any place he could. He had to pound on two more with his gun and punch yet another in the face before the others got the message that he would be one hell of a hard man to get past.

"CB Wooly," he called, once he had the mob in hand, "Are you alive or dead?"

Danner had just enough time to start worrying before he got word that CB Wooly had in some amazing way bested Clay Bardoe.

****

Wooly didn't move a muscle for the longest time, standing still in the exact spot from which he'd fired his two rounds. All the time he stood there, he stared at the table in the far back corner and the man pushed into the wall whose face he thankfully could not see. All that time he maintained a tight grip on his gun, but had dropped his shooting hand down alongside his body. He didn't seem to have the strength to raise it, so he lowered his head to look down at both. At that instance he realized he was standing on the same spot of floor that Dallas Babb died on. Although he took no pride whatsoever in what he'd just done, it astounded him that, like Clay Bardoe, he placed a killing shot at a distance of over fifty paces. Of course, it took him two tries to Clay's one, but CB Wooly never claimed to be even near the marksman that his old partner had been.

Once he finally eased his gun back in the holster, Wooly started the long trek from Babb's blood stains to Bardoe's body. He had just rounded the side of the table closest to the slumped form, when he felt something small and hard through the sole of his right boot. He raised his foot to spot the object and noticed it was one of many which were scattered along the floor beside and beneath the table.

From where he stood, Wooly began counting and when he spotted a tenth, he quickly bent and scooped up Bardoe's closest pistol. He thumbed open the gate on the right side of the cylinder, pulled the hammer back to the second click and rotated the cylinder with his thumb. What he discovered caused him to toss the gun onto the table top and then practically dive beneath it to retrieve the other Colt. An inspection of that gun revealed the same thing. All twelve cylinder chambers on the Colts were empty. The bullets lay scattered across the floor at Bardoe's feet.

Wooly stood upright and sighed hard before looking down at the remains of a damned good friend and even a better partner. "Clay, you son of a bitch! You emptied your guns. You made me kill you."

After many moments of struggling, with both his conscience and a cornucopia of emotions, Wooly gave into plain old pride. He bent on one knee, scooped up twelve unspent .45 caliber rounds and loaded Bardoe's pistols. When he finished, he positioned each on the floor beneath a dangling hand.

He did not tarry a moment longer. Wooly strode the length of fifty plus paces to and through the swinging doors and tried to ignore the inner accusations of scandalous behavior.

****

By the time Wooly stepped out of the Drovers, Danner had managed to disperse the curious onlookers. Only a couple of more tried to get around him. Like their predecessors, they left with help from friends and acquaintances. The rest finally accepted the fact they would not be going into the saloon until the short and very sturdy man stepped aside.

Danner felt damned near exhausted, and Wooly looked the same, maybe even worse. About the same moment Wooly walked out, town Marshal Gray Wilson and two of his deputies stepped up on the walkway.

"Glad you could make it, Marshal Wilson," Wooly deadpanned.

"Glad you are still standing, Marshal Wooly," Wilson grinned, not considering Wooly's remark less than complimentary.

"May we go in and take a look see?" Wilson then asked Wooly.

"It's your town."

Once the three made it past them and into the Drover's, Wooly turned his head toward Danner. "You want to go take a gander?"

Danner shook his head. "Although he helped put me in prison, I was rather fond of Clay Bardoe. Don't particularly care to see him dead."

Both men stood silently for several seconds looking at the world out in front of them. Finally, Danner deemed it all just too damned quiet.

"I'm headed west. So long, CB Wooly."

"What if being on the right side of the law don't work out for you?" Wooly asked.

"Well, I can't do no worse on the right side than I did on the wrong side. But, if I can't make a go of it, I got another plan. I figure I'll join Bill Cody's Wild West Show."

Wooly turned a surprised, if not impressed, look on Danner. "Floyd, I didn't know you was either a trick rider or a shootist."

"Well, I ain't neither," Danner admitted.

"Then what the hell do you hope to do in old Wild Bill's shows?"

"I've been told he can't get enough Indians and that he'll hire white men to act like Indians. I'll be blamed if I can't act like a wild Indian!"

Wooly just shook his head and worked up a smile, but it seemed to come real hard. He extended his shaking hand toward Danner.

"Thanks for standing by me today. I will not soon forget that."

Danner shook the hand and turned to leave, but then paused and gave into a burning curiosity. "CB, how the hell did you win this fight today?"

Danner could tell the man before him, who doubtlessly would soon be considered a living legend, struggled mightily for a response.

It took him a long while, but CB Wooly finally cocked his head and replied, "Floyd, the God-honest truth is that Clay Bardoe was just not as interested as I was in winning this fight."

Floyd Danner walked away from CB Wooly thinking hard about those last words. He concentrated on the meaning for the entire two blocks he walked in order to reach his horse. Once he saddled up, he rode back to the Drover's, and found Wooly still standing on the sidewalk staring hard at a bare and empty spot on the dirt street out in front of the saloon.

"CB," Danner said as he reined to a stop, "what you told me didn't explain a damned thing."

Wooly never looked up from whatever invisible sight held his attention. He just nodded his head a couple of times and replied, "Ain't that the truth?"

Acknowledgments

Because these contributors are all so very dear to me and equally important to the outcome of this novel, I've listed them in alphabetical order.

To Kristen Remington, my administrative assistant, your technical skills and patience, make my life much better. You are a gem.

To Henry P. (Pat) Scully of Scully Associates, many thanks for your remarkable cover design.

SD Shelton, a fellow author, I sincerely appreciate your guidance and inspiration.

Finally to my tenacious editor, David Shupe, my work couldn't be what it is without your guidance and editing skills. Thank you.

About the Author

Keith Remer is a retired Army colonel and an adjunct professor of history. He has to date written twelve novels and is the recipient of the *International Indy Book Award for Fiction* for his novel, *The Hiding Place of Thunder.*

Keith lives in rural Oklahoma City on his beloved Honey Lee Ranch with any stray dog that comes along. He occasionally gets thrown from his horse but has survived in order to tell his tales.

Killling Bardow is Book One in *The Calamitous Breed* trilogy. Look for Book Two, *Blood City,* coming in Summer of 2018.

To connect with the author, visit his Facebook page @KeithRemerAuthor